I0753355

The Librarian of Bertiswil

H.M. Medeiros

ISBN 979-8-9933491-2-1

plumeriatreepress@gmail.com

For my great-great-grandparents,

whose quiet lives of goodness and struggle

inspired this story

Author's Note

While some Swiss German and High German words are briefly defined within the text, **all others appear in the alphabetical glossary at the back**, following the Historical Afterword and Note to the Reader. There you'll find definitions, cultural notes, and phonetic approximations in English for the remaining words and phrases.

English translations for the song lyrics follow the glossary.

Chapter One
The Girl Who Climbed Trees and Read Books

Elisabetha Villiger was not cut out to be a farmer's daughter. Not in the *Kanton* of Aargau in Switzerland, not in the first decades of the nineteenth century, when the land still bore the scars of Napoleonic passage and the old ways clung like frost to the fields. That much was certain by the time she turned eight, when her parents had already made clear that she was a disappointment to them.

She had been born deep in the Aargauer countryside in 1802, far outside the hamlet of Geltwil, where the church bells marked time more faithfully than any clock, and where farmers' daughters were expected to peel potatoes, darn socks, and marry young. But Elisabetha hated most everything about farm life. She hated the churn of butter, the stink of sausage casings, the sticky heat of the smokehouse. She hated the way the cellar swallowed light and the barn pressed in with its sour breath. She hated the rhythm of farm life—the endless repetition of tasks that never seemed to matter.

She preferred books. And silence.

Her mother, Appollonia, watched her from the kitchen window, beefy forearms elbow-deep in pork fat, as the girl climbed the pear tree again. A book was tucked under her arm, its pages fluttering like wings. Appollonia sighed and turned back to the sausage. "*Sie isch nid wie di andere,*" she murmured.

Her father, Johann, stood sharpening his scythe outside the barn. He glanced up once, squinting at his daughter's figure in the branches. "*Ungeschickt,*" he muttered. Clumsy. "Big-boned, bookish, and no use to anyone."

It was true that she was big-boned, with heavy-lidded blue eyes and a square figure that made her look older than her years. Her eyesight was poor, and she squinted at the pages of *Der Schweizerische Beobachter*, a borrowed pamphlet from the village schoolmaster. She read about Napoleon's retreat and wondered what it would feel like to lose everything.

She was always supposed to be doing something useful around the farm. Boiling apple butter. Or picking fruit. Or helping her mother with the sausage. But instead she climbed trees and dreamed of libraries.

She didn't particularly care about the Napoleonic battles. She cared about the words. The way they bent and shimmered. The way they made her feel like she was somewhere else.

"*Lisbeth!*" her mother called shrilly. This was the name her parents called her at home. "Come down from there! The butter won't churn itself!"

The quiet girl almost never spoke, but she shot a mildly annoyed look in her mother's direction as if to say, "*Don't bother me. Can't you see I'm reading?*"

One autumn afternoon, Elisabetha climbed the pear tree again. Its leaves were gold and brittle. She opened her book and read aloud to the wind. Her father watched from a field and shook his head.

"You'll never marry a farmer," Papa muttered, not loudly, but loud enough for her to hear. This was a heavy criticism, indeed. Elisabetha was descended from a modest family of Swiss Catholic *Bauernleute*—smallholding farming people—in the *Kanton* of Aargau that stretched back in time for hundreds of years, their lives rooted in soil and sacrament.

Slowly she climbed down, brushed the bark from her skirt, and went into the big farm kitchen. The house always smelled of vinegar and smoke. The hearth was always lit. Butter was churned in a wooden barrel with a squeaking handle. Strings of fatty sausages hung from the rafters. The cellar held apples, potatoes, carrots, and the sour smell of fermenting cabbage. Elisabetha hated it all. Her mother pointed to the butter barrel. She began to churn without speaking.

That night, the girl read by candlelight in the cellar. She sat on a crate of apples and turned the pages slowly, savoring each sentence like a taste of rare honey. Upstairs, her parents argued in low voices. She heard her name. She heard the words "*alti Jungfer.*" She heard the word "worthless."

Her throat tightened, but she did not cry. She would be a burden. A disappointment. She carried those words like a stone in her pocket, certain they were true.

Elisabetha felt shame, but also a small, stubborn defiance. She knew she was not beautiful. She knew she was not particularly useful. But she also knew that books spoke to her in ways people did not.

The girl prayed at night, not for a husband, but for a life that made sense.

She dreamed of cities. Of libraries. Of men who spoke gently and knew Latin and ancient Greek.

She was twelve when she first heard the words "old maid." She was fourteen when she decided she would never marry a man who couldn't read. At fifteen, Elisabetha began to hide in the barn loft with her books. She built a nest of hay and old blankets and read until her fingers went numb. Her mother found her once and scolded her for ruining her eyesight. Her father found her another time and said nothing, just shook his head and walked away.

"She'll never marry," Appollonia clucked yet again.

"She'll never be a farmer's wife," Johann lamented for the hundredth time.

Her mother scolded her gently. Her father scolded her less gently. But they never beat her. They simply worried.

Finally, they stopped trying to change her.

Chapter Two
The Librarian of Sins

At sixteen, Elisabetha's parents began to badger her to attend the church dances in Geltwil and Benzenschwil. She stood awkwardly near the wall while the other girls laughed and twirled. Her dress was plain. Her figure square. Her eyes squinted behind the wire-rimmed spectacles she had worn since the age of ten. No one asked her to dance.

She went home and read until dawn.

At twenty-six, she was still unmarried. The villagers whispered. Her parents no longer even discussed their daughter's lack of matrimonial prospects. She helped with the chores, but only the ones that didn't involve blood or brine. She prayed in the mornings and read in the evenings. She was quiet. She was obedient. But she felt abnormal. Out of place.

Though rather tall, her figure was ungainly—as if the top half of her did not belong to the bottom. She had a pair of bird-like legs and flat hips, a thick waist and thin arms, broad shoulders, and an ample bosom below a short neck. Her face was broad, with prominent cheek and jaw bones, blue eyes that held a quiet clarity, and mousy brown hair that refused to hold a curl. Her complexion was pale—not porcelain, but the kind of pallor earned from years indoors with books, not sun. In summer, she freckled across the nose and cheekbones, but the color never held. Her skin had a matte quality, like unglazed clay.

She did not envy the pretty girls, not exactly. But she knew how they were looked at, and how she was not. It made her quieter. It made her careful.

Elisabetha knew what she was. She had long accepted that her life would be small, the kind that passed without notice, and she had learned to live inside her own thoughts, where the books she read gave her room to breathe.

Then, at another village dance, she met Josef Moser. He was tall—almost gangly—bespectacled, serious-looking, with a narrow face and a voice like polished wood. She learned that he was the librarian of the town of Sins.

Elisabetha had developed a habit of carrying a small folded pamphlet or book in her cloth reticule, which she would pull out and read clandestinely in her lap as she sat in her accustomed place on the sidelines.

She was startled when the tall man approached her and asked what she was reading. She told him. He nodded. Then he asked what she thought of the pamphlet's argument about the Holy Roman Empire. She answered. His lips twitched upward, the ghost of a smile.

He asked her name. "Elisabetha Villiger," she answered, in a voice that was just above a hush.

Things moved quickly after this first meeting. Elisabetha and Josef married far too quickly for her parents' tastes. They were skeptical. "He's not a farmer," Johann grumbled. "He's not one of us."

"He's a man of books," Elisabetha countered. "He understands me."

Appollonia looked at her daughter's square figure and weak eyes and said nothing. She did not want to say what she was thinking. But she could not help wondering what a formally educated townsman like Josef Moser would see in her child, the daughter of practically illiterate *Bauernleute* from the middle of nowhere in the Aargauer countryside. In those days, Catholic farmers had no need for much book learning. Most could cipher a fair bit and make their marks. They did not read the Bible, instead relying on the village priest to relay the Word of God during Mass. But the Villigers' daughter had practically come out of her mother's womb reading, so they had done what they could for her education.

The wedding took place in early spring, when the fields were still bare and the wind carried the smell of thawing earth. It was a small Catholic ceremony in the Altstadt of Sins, held in the seventeenth century Kirche Sankt Antonius, with its gray stone walls, ancient wooden crucifix, and cracked plaster saints. The bride wore her best clothes: a white blouse with large puffed sleeves beneath a blue wool bodice and skirt, a starched linen cap and apron, a black tatted lace shawl drawn over her shoulders, and knitted stockings with black leather boots. She carried a small bouquet of *Margueritli*, her rosary, and prayer book. The groom wore a dark suit, a silver cravat, knee breeches, silk stockings, and silver-buckled shoes.

Her parents had traveled to Sins from the farm for the occasion. Johann Villiger wore his best jacket, which smelled faintly of manure and pipe smoke. Appollonia Villiger had scrubbed her hands raw the night before, but the scent of sausage still clung to her skin. They looked ruddy and out of place among the townsfolk—their hobnailed boots heavy, their faces weathered, their silence thick.

The Villigers stood stiffly in the front pew, watching their daughter with unreadable expressions.

After the priest had spoken somberly of duty and obedience, and then pronounced the couple man and wife, Elisabetha turned to her parents, hopeful. Her mother approached and kissed her once on the cheek, dry-lipped and brief. Her father shook Josef Moser's hand without a word, his grip firm but not warm.

Then Elisabetha's parents climbed back into their horse cart, the wheels creaking as they turned toward the Aargauer countryside. She watched them go from the chapel steps, her shawl pulled tight around her shoulders. The wind nearly lifted her starched white cap from her head, despite it being tied securely under her chin with a silk ribbon. Josef Moser stood beside her, hands in the pockets of his dark suit, glassy eyes fixed on the cobblestones.

He did not once take his bride's hand.

The newly married couple's wedding supper at a nearby inn was modest. There was bread, cheese, new cider, and a roast chicken that Josef barely touched. He spoke little to his new wife. She tried to catch his eye once, but he looked past her, as if she were a shadow cast by someone else.

After the serving maid cleared the dishes, he stood, left some coins on the table, and said, "Come. I'll show you the house."

They walked in silence through the cobbled streets of Sins, past shuttered shops and the darkened church. The librarian's house was narrow and tall, with a steep roof and a small brass knocker shaped like a lion's head. He opened the door and stepped aside to let his wife inside.

The front room smelled of ink and dust. Books lined every wall—stacked on shelves, piled on tables, even resting on the windowsills like sleeping cats. Elisabetha's heart lifted. She had never seen so many volumes in one place. She reached out her gloved hand to touch a leather-bound spine, but Josef cleared his throat.

"This way."

He led her up the narrow staircase, past a closed door on the left and into a small room at the end of the hall. She noticed immediately that her carved wooden trunk and leather satchel containing all of her possessions had been placed inside. The chamber held a single bed, a small night table on which sat an oil lamp, washstand, and a black wooden crucifix nailed to the wall. A folded goose down quilt sat at the foot of the bed. The mullioned window looked out into the street.

"This will be your bedroom," he said.

She turned to him in surprise. "And yours?"

He gestured vaguely toward the closed door. "I keep irregular hours. It's better this way."

She nodded, unsure what else to say.

He did not kiss her goodnight. He did not touch her hand. He simply turned and walked away, his footsteps fading down the stairs.

Elisabetha sat on the edge of the bed and looked around. The black crucifix stared back at her. The quilt lay flat and undisturbed. The silence was complete.

In the next heartbeat, she understood that she would never share a bed with her husband.

And she would never truly be his wife.

Chapter Three
The Marriage of Silence

At first, it felt like freedom.

No butter to churn. No sausages to stuff. No floors to scrub. Elisabetha woke each morning to the smell of coffee she hadn't brewed and bread she hadn't baked. The housekeeper, a quiet woman named Marta, came and went with the rhythm of a metronome—sweeping, scrubbing, boiling, folding, without comment. There was a cook, too, who prepared meals with a precision that made Elisabetha feel both grateful and useless.

She wandered the house like a ghost with no chores.

Josef Moser had said she could read anything in his library. And she did. She read pamphlets on theology, treatises on history, volumes of poetry so dense she had to reread each line three times. She read until her eyes ached and her fingers smelled of ink and old paper. She read to fill the hours and the silence.

Goethe first—*Die Leiden des jungen Werthers*—which made her weep, though she wasn't sure if it was for Werther or herself. Then Schiller, whose dramas stirred something fierce and unspoken in her. She read *Wilhelm Tell* twice, then once more aloud, just to hear the words echo in the stillness of the house.

She read Homer in a German translation, tracing her finger along the lines of *The Odyssey*, imagining herself not as Penelope but as Odysseus—wandering, clever, always searching for a home that did not exist.

She even read Shakespeare, though it was foreign and strange, even in German translation. *Macbeth* unsettled her. *Hamlet* made her ache. She underlined a soliloquy in pencil and stared at it for days:

To be, or not to be? That is the question—
Whether 'tis nobler in the mind to suffer
The slings and arrows of outrageous fortune,
Or to take arms against a sea of troubles,
And, by opposing, end them? To die, to sleep—
No more—and by a sleep to say we end
The heart-ache and the thousand natural shocks
That flesh is heir to—'tis a consummation
Devoutly to be wish'd. To die, to sleep—
To sleep, perchance to dream—ay, there's the rub…

She read the lines again, lips barely moving. Then she closed the book and stared at the window, where the frost had begun to lace the corners of the glass. The words clung to her like breath in cold air.

To die, to sleep.

It sounded so gentle. So clean. As if death could be folded away like a nightgown.

But perchance to dream—that was the terror. That even in death, the ache might follow. That silence might not be an end, but an echo.

She thought of Josef, of the way he moved through the house without touching anything. Of the way he never looked at her. She thought of the cook's eyes filled with pity, of her housekeeper's whispers, of the ache that had no name.

She was not suicidal. But she understood now what it meant to endure—not from courage, but from uncertainty. And she understood, too, the difficulty of enduring when the pain to do so was almost unbearable.

She opened the book again and underscored the line with a steady hand: *Thus conscience does make cowards of us all.*

Josef never asked what she was reading.

Because Josef did not speak to her.

He nodded at her in the mornings. He passed her in the hallway. He sometimes sat across from her at supper, eating slowly, methodically, without looking up. When she asked him questions—about a book, about the weather, about anything—he answered in one or two words, or not at all.

She told herself he was busy. That he was tired. That he was simply a quiet man.

But the silence grew teeth.

One afternoon, she stood in the library doorway and watched him shelve a book. He moved with care, aligning the spine perfectly with the others. She stepped inside.

"I finished *Wilhelm Tell*," she said softly. "I keep thinking about the moment Tell refuses to bow to Gessler's hat. Do you think most Swiss people would have done the same?"

Josef turned slightly, his face unreadable. "It's only a play," he said.

"Yes," she said. "But it feels true."

He said nothing.

"I also read *Werther*. I wonder if despair is a kind of cry for help. What do you think?"

He slid another book into place and turned back to the shelf. "I'm working."

She stood there a moment longer, then left.

The thrill of domestic freedom wore off by the third month. She had no farm work, no children to care for, no duties beyond existing. She tried embroidery. She tried baking. She tried writing letters to her parents, but the words felt hollow, and besides, she knew they would struggle to read them.

One morning, Elisabetha came down early. The house was still dim, the shutters drawn against the pale light. She moved softly, her slippers silent on the tiled floor. In the kitchen, she heard voices—low, hurried, not meant for her.

Marta, the housekeeper, was speaking in hushed tones. The cook, a stout woman named Therese, responded with a cluck of sympathy.

"*Sie tuet mer leid*," Marta whispered. "*So ganz allei. Und er isch immer so chalt.*"

Therese sighed and then shrugged. "*Ich glaub, er het sie nie welle.*"

Elisabetha stood just outside the doorway, her breath caught in her throat. Even her servants felt sorry for her. But why would Josef have married her, if he had not wanted her? It made no sense.

She stepped back, careful not to make a sound. Her heart thudded in her chest. She returned to the hallway and waited a moment before entering the kitchen with deliberate footsteps.

"*Guete Morge*," she announced briskly.

Both women turned quickly. Therese busied herself with the bread basket. Both women's faces flushed scarlet with the knowledge of being overheard.

"*Guete Morge*, *Frau* Moser," Marta said, too brightly.

Elisabetha nodded and sat at the table. The bread was warm. The butter was fresh. The silence was unbearable.

She did not speak of what she'd overheard. She did not ask for kindness. She simply ate, slowly, and returned to the library.

Later that day, she opened *Hamlet* again and reread the line: *I have that within which passeth show.*

She underlined it twice. Some kinds of sorrow lived too deep for display.

She began to walk the streets of Sins alone, nodding to neighbors who barely knew her. She attended Mass daily at the Kirche Sankt Antonius and lit candles. At first she told herself they were for the poor souls in purgatory, but deep down, she knew she lit them for herself. She sat in her pew and prayed for clarity, for companionship, for something she could name.

At night, Elisabetha lay in her narrow bed and listened to the sounds of the house—the creak of floorboards, the tick of the grandfather clock, the distant rustle of pages turning in the room down the hall.

She wondered what he read. She wondered what he thought. She wondered if he ever thought of her.

Years passed this way. One evening, she dared to raise the subject.

They sat at supper, Marta having served breaded pork cutlets, boiled potatoes, and peas. Josef ate slowly, perfunctorily, as always.

Elisabetha cleared her throat. "Josef," she asked timidly. "Have I offended you in some way?"

He looked up, startled.

"I only ask because…we live as strangers. It has been going on this way for twelve years now, since the day of our marriage."

He said nothing. His eyes were glued to his plate.

She pressed on. The next question would be awkward to speak aloud. "Is there something displeasing to you about my person?"

His facial expression twisted into a grimace. He pulled the linen napkin from his lap and threw it on the table. Without a word, he stood and left the room.

She sat alone, the pork cutlet cooling on her plate, the ache in her chest growing sharper. She never asked again.

Elisabetha filled her days with books and silence. She memorized the titles on the shelves, the patterns on the wallpaper, the sound of Josef's footsteps on the stairs. She prayed more often. She stopped writing letters altogether.

She did not cry.

She simply endured.

Chapter Four
The River

It was Therese who answered the door.

Elisabetha heard the knock from upstairs—a sharp, urgent sound that did not belong to the late hour. She had already changed into her nightgown and was brushing out her hair when she heard the servant's footsteps cross the tiled floor.

A murmur of voices. Then a pause.

"*Frau* Moser?" Therese's voice trembled. "It's the constable. He says he must speak with you."

Elisabetha stood. Her brush slipped from her fingers and clattered to the floor.

"Tell him I'll be down in a moment," she said, her voice steadier than she felt.

She dressed quickly, her fingers clumsy with the buttons. Marta appeared without a word and helped her lace up her bodice.

When she descended the stairs, the constable was waiting in the entryway, hat in hand. He looked uncomfortable, his eyes fixed on the floor.

"*Frau* Moser," he said, bowing slightly. "I regret to inform you…your husband's body has been found."

She stared at him, thunderstruck.

She heard her own voice, as if it were coming from a faraway place. "Where?"

"On the banks of the Reuss. Just outside town."

"He was *in* the river?" Her voice was barely audible.

He nodded. "I'm afraid so."

"But…he couldn't swim." She had heard it once, from someone who'd known Josef as a boy.

"I'm sorry," he said again. "We'll need you to come to the *Totenstube.* To identify his body."

Marta must have been listening at the door, for suddenly she appeared with her mistress's heavy black hooded cape, the one that was fur-lined, and wrapped her in it. Then she offered her the leather gloves.

The carriage ride was a blur of narrow streets and lanterns. The horse's hooves struck the cobblestones like nails into wood. Elisabetha sat stiffly beside the constable, hands clenched in her lap, cape pulled tightly around her, the fur damp from the moist night air. The cold seeped through the seams of the carriage, and she felt it in her teeth.

She did not speak. Neither did he.

Elisabetha had never been in the streets at this hour. The town looked different in the dark—hollow, stripped of its shape. No bakery smells. No children playing hopscotch on the cobblestones. Just mist, darkness, and silence.

The *Totenstube* was a squat building behind the church, its windows shuttered like eyes that refused to see. A lantern burned above the door, casting a yellow bruise on the wall.

Inside, the air was thick with the scents of lye, damp linen, and some sickeningly sweet odor she could not identify—something that clung to her lungs.

The magistrate was waiting. He was a small man with a bulbous red nose and a voice like gravel. He did not bow. He did not smile.

"You're the wife?" he barked.

She nodded.

"This way."

She followed him down a narrow corridor. Lit torches set into the stone walls flickered and cast ghastly shadows. The floor was wet.

The body lay on a table, covered in a coarse white sheet. The man pulled it back without ceremony.

It was Josef.

His face was grotesquely bloated, the skin so pale as to be nearly translucent. His spectacles were missing. His mouth hung open, as if mid- scream. His eyes appeared squeezed shut. His dark hair was matted to his scalp. One hand was clenched. The other was loose.

She did not cry. She did not speak.

"So. Is it him?" the magistrate asked bluntly.

She nodded.

"Could he swim?"

"No."

"Do you have any idea why he might have been there or what might have happened?"

She shook her head, tears welling up in her eyes.

The constable who stood near the wall shifted his weight. "It appears your husband drowned himself, *Frau* Moser. I am sorry."

Her eyes gazed upon Josef's face one final time.

Then she turned away and began to retch into her handkerchief. The room tilted, and she swayed. The constable reached out to steady her, but she shook him off.

"I'd like to go home now," she said quietly.

The next morning, Elisabetha dressed in silence.

She chose a black dress with a high, stiff collar and long sleeves that brushed her hands. Marta wordlessly helped her fasten the hooks, her hands gentle. Then she laid out the gloves and cape without being asked.

Elisabetha could not eat. She did not speak.

Then she walked—alone—through the Altstadt, past the bakery, past the cobbler, past the square where children played. The frost had not yet melted. Her boots struck the cobblestones like a metronome.

She passed through the town without a word. Eyes followed her. Mouths moved behind closed fingers. Shutters snapped shut on windows.

She walked to the Kirche Sankt Antonius, the old Catholic church with its age-darkened crucifix and bell tower that had rung for the past two hundred years for births, baptisms, and weddings—including her own.

The rectory door was heavy oak, carved with vines and haloed saints whose faces seemed to glare at her. Elisabetha knocked once, then waited. The frost clung to her gloves. Her breath hung in the air like smoke.

A young sacristan opened the door. He looked at her black cape, her stiff collar, her face drained of sleep.

"I need to speak with the *Herr Pfarrer*," she said, her voice steady.

He regarded her with sad eyes, nodded, and led her down a narrow corridor. The walls were lined with oil-darkened paintings of people who had never smiled.

The pastor was seated at a desk beneath a worn wooden crucifix. A single candle burned beside him. He did not rise when Elisabetha entered the room.

"*Frau* Moser," he stated flatly. "I've heard."

She remained standing. "I've come to make the arrangements for my husband."

He looked at her for a long moment. Then he closed the book in front of him.

"Your husband took his own life."

She pretended as if she did not understand him. "He couldn't swim."

"Then why would he have been at the river at all? And especially during winter?"

She swallowed hard. "What are you saying?"

"I cannot possibly bury him."

"*Please.*" The word tore from her lips, a fiercely whispered plea.

"Impossible."

She stared at him. His face was calm, almost bored.

"You must accept the fact that he is in hell and will spend all of eternity there, *Frau* Moser. And his body will not pollute our sacred ground."

Elisabetha's throat tightened.

"*He was your parishioner.*"

"He has committed the gravest of all mortal sins, I am sorry to say. God will not have mercy upon his soul."

She did not cry. And she would not plead for him again.

She rose, turned, and walked out.

The sad-eyed sacristan watched her go, his hands folded like a child who had learned not to ask questions. He followed her to the door and opened it.

Elisabetha did not know what to do.

The Catholic church had closed its doors to her. The *Herr Pfarrer* had spoken of hell, of polluted ground, of sin that could not be forgiven. There had been no room for compassion. Only judgment.

She returned home and sat at the kitchen table for hours, her gloves still on, the cape draped over her shoulders like a shroud. Marta brought her a cup of tea. Therese lit the stove. No one spoke.

She had heard—in whispers, in stories not meant for her ears—that Catholics sometimes turned to the Swiss Reformed Church when suicide struck a family. It was not encouraged. It was not spoken of. But it happened. This Protestant denomination had been founded in the sixteenth century by the theologian Huldrych Zwingli.

The Villiger family had been Catholic for hundreds of years. Baptized, married, buried in the same rites. The idea of crossing that line felt like an unspeakable betrayal.

But Josef was dead. And the consecrated ground of their church would not be opened for him.

So Elisabetha rose from the kitchen table, raised the hood of her cape, and went in search of the town's Protestant church.

The building was small and plain. No saints. No stained glass windows. No tabernacle. No incense. Just a pulpit, a plain wooden table, polished wooden benches, and silence.

She knocked at the roughly hewn side door.

The pastor opened it himself. He was a man in his fifties, with a lined face and hands that looked like they had chopped wood. He did not wear a white collar. Just a dark woolen neckcloth with his homespun suit.

"I am *Frau* Elisabetha Moser," she whispered, her voice barely audible.

He nodded and took her hand. "I am *Pfarrer* Graf. Please come in," he said gently.

The study was warm. A fire burned low in the grate. Books lined the walls. A Bible lay open on the desk.

He invited Elisabetha to sit and then joined her.

"My husband is dead," she stated simply.

He waited.

"They found him on the banks of the Reuss."

He nodded once. "I've heard," he responded quietly. "I'm very sorry for your loss."

She ignored his condolences. "They say he drowned himself."

"I see."

"The Catholic church will not bury him."

"I know."

She looked down at her gloves. "I don't know what to do."

"You've come here."

"Yes. I don't know why he did it," she whispered, her eyes lowered in shame.

"We do not need to know why he did it," he said without hesitation. "Only that he did. And that you grieve."

She swallowed the colossal lump that had sprung up in her throat. She could barely whisper the words. "Will you bury him?"

"*Ja*."

She looked up. An expression of compassion suffused the man's face.

"Our God is merciful, *Frau* Moser. How, then, can I not show mercy to others, no matter what they have done?" *Pfarrer* Graf asked kindly.

She did not cry. But something in her chest loosened.

"We will hold a small graveside service, and he will be laid to rest in our cemetery," he said. "My wife will attend. Perhaps one or two others. It will be quiet."

She nodded.

"*Danke vilmal.*" Elisabetha could barely choke out the words. They seemed so small and insignificant.

He bowed his head. "You are welcome, *Frau* Moser. May his soul rest in peace."

That night, after the house had gone still, Elisabetha lit a single candle and sat at Josef's desk.

The mourning dress still clung to her like damp wool. She had not eaten. Her gloves lay folded beside the inkwell.

She pulled a sheet of parchment from the drawer and smoothed it flat. The pen hesitated in her hand.

She began to write.

Dear Mama and Papa,

Josef is dead.

They found him on the banks of the Reuss. It was unexpected.
I was not prepared.
I am alone now. The house is quiet.
If it is not too great a burden, I ask to return home. I promise I will not be idle. I will help where I can.
Please let me know if I may come, and I will begin to pack. There is much to sort through.
Your daughter,
Elisabetha Moser

She read it twice. She stared at the words. They looked too small for the enormity of what had happened. But she could not write more. There was no mention of what really happened at the river. No mention of the Catholic pastor's refusal or what kind of service there would be.

She folded the letter, sealed it with wax, and placed it by the door for the morning post.

Then she sat in the dark, the candle guttering low, and listened to the stove creak as it cooled.

The morning of the burial service was bitter. Elisabetha did not ask, nor did she expect, the servants to attend.

Frost clung to the grass in the Protestant cemetery, turning the ground to glass. The sky was the color of tin. No birds sang.

She stood beside the grave, her cape pulled tight, her gloves stiff with cold. *Pfarrer* Graf was there, his woolen scarf tucked into his coat. His wife stood next to the widow, hands folded, eyes lowered. The gravedigger stood at a respectful distance, cap in hand, shovel at the ready.

The coffin rested above the open earth. It was plain pine, unvarnished. No flowers. No cross.

The pastor cleared his throat.

"We are gathered," he said, "not to judge, but to lay Josef Moser to rest."

His voice was quiet, but it carried.

"God's mercy is not earned," he said. "It is given freely."

Then he read the Twenty-Third Psalm from his open Bible:

> *The Lord is my shepherd; I shall not want.*
> *He makes me lie down in green pastures.*
> *He leads me beside still waters.*
> *He restores my soul.*
> *He leads me in paths of righteousness for his name's sake.*
> *Even though I walk through the valley of the shadow of death,*
> *I will fear no evil, for you are with me;*
> *your rod and your staff, they comfort me…*

When he was finished reading, the pastor nodded to the gravedigger.

The ropes were pulled. The box descended.

The earth waited to receive it.

Then he nodded slightly toward the widow. Elisabetha stepped forward.

She bent, scooped a handful of cold dirt from the mound beside the grave, and let it fall onto the coffin. It struck the wood with a soft thud.

The pastor's wife followed. Her gesture was smaller, more tentative. The dirt slipped through her fingers like ash.

They turned.

A young man with a darkened expression stood far behind them. His blazing eyes met theirs, and for a moment, they held.

He did not step forward.

He did not speak.

He simply glared at them, jaw clenched, eyes burning with something that looked like contempt.

Then he looked away.

When Elisabetha turned to look for the young man again, he was gone.

She stood unmoving until the final shovelful of dirt fell, her cheeks marked by frozen trails of tears.

She would not cry for Josef Moser from that moment on. Never again.

Chapter Five
Rupture and Revelation

The letter came on a Tuesday. It was just a folded scrap of paper written by her mother and stuffed into a tiny gray envelope. She knew this because her father could not write at all. "*Liebe Tochter, komm jetzt heim,*" it read.

Relief spread through her, dull and numbing. She read the letter twice, then laid it on the table beside the stove. It stayed there for days, until the paper began to curl at the edges.

When she finally began to pack, the silence was thick. Marta and Therese arrived with wooden crates and twine, but they did not offer much help. They did not know how to dismantle Josef Moser's life, either.

It was all on her. Every item. Every shelf. Every drawer. She had never been expected to do such things before. Not as a daughter. Not as a wife. And now the whole house was hers to empty and sell.

She stood in the library doorway and felt the wind go out of her.

It was not a small library. Not a shelf or two, but an entire room lined from floor to ceiling with volumes—Aeschylus, Ovid, Shakespeare, Goethe, for a start. Plays. Poetry. Histories. Atlases. A full set of encyclopedias. The philosophy and teachings of Socrates, Plato, and Aristotle. A copy of the Gutenberg Bible. Books were rare. Costly. Precious. She had dreamed of owning even just a few since she was a girl.

And now she owned an entire library.

Elisabetha swaddled each book in linen, slowly and carefully, as if she were swaddling an infant. She tied each one with string and laid them in wooden crates and trunks. Her breath came shallow. Her hands shook. But she continued until the final volume was packed and the shelves were bare.

One sleepless night, a sudden impulse seized Elisabetha to go to the river that took her husband. She left before dawn the following morning.

The frost had crusted the fields and the sky hung low, colorless. No birds. No wind. Just the sound of her boots on the road.

The Reuss lay east of Sins, past the last stone house and a ditch where cows probably used to drink. On this morning, it moved slow, thick, like a boa constrictor digesting. The banks were hard with ice. The reeds brittle. Elisabetha walked until the air changed—until the cold felt sharper, the silence heavier. This was the place. No one had shown it to her. She simply knew.

The river did not shimmer. It did not mourn. It moved like a beast with no eyes. It had taken her husband. Swallowed him whole. And now it kept moving in its maddening slowness, as if nothing had happened.

She stood at the edge.

The water folded over itself, gray and slow. It did not speak. It did not stop.

She did not cry, but her knees gave way. She knelt on top of the frost, her gloves soaked through, her breath shallow. The river kept moving.

It had taken him. That was all.

That night, sleep escaped Elisabetha yet again.

The fire had gone out in the grate in her bedroom. She lay beneath the quilt with her eyes wide open, watching the ceiling fade from gray to black. Her breath clouded in the cold. Her hands were folded on her chest like a corpse.

In the wee hours, she finally rose and pulled on her dressing gown, thinking she might as well get some more work done, instead of just staring at the ceiling until morning.

She lit no lamp, moving through the dark by memory. Down the hall. Down the stairs. Past the kitchen. Into the library.

Josef's *Biedermeier* desk stood waiting, squat and heavy. It was cherry wood, polished to a dull sheen, with clean lines and brass pulls that caught the lamplight. No ornament. No flourish. Just order.

It had always been his domain. She had never opened a single one of its drawers. Now she would open them all. She had dusted it days ago but left it for last. Elisabetha knew the desk would take a great deal of time to sort through, so she decided now was as good a time as any to make a start.

She lit a lamp and sat.

The drawers were full. Receipts. Letters. Notes written in his hand. She began to sort them into piles—what to keep, what to burn. She worked slowly, methodically, her fingers numb from the cold and the weight of it all.

The last drawer was deeper than the others. She emptied it, laid the papers flat, and reached up to feel along the joints. Her hand had caught on something that seemed to be stuck to the bottom of the drawer above it.

She examined it more closely. There, affixed to the underside of the next-to-last drawer, attached with two brass tacks, was a thick folder. Bound with rough twine. She pried it loose, laid it on the desk, and stared at its title for several long seconds.

Homoerotische Kunstwerke.

She blinked. The words meant nothing at first, even though her Latin and German were strong.

Then they did.

She untied the twine and opened the cover. Inside were at least twenty pen and ink prints of men. Naked men.

The first image depicted a male couple, their bodies joined together in a way that made her breath catch. She turned to the next print and looked at it. Then the next. And the next one after that.

Elisabetha broke out in a cold sweat. Her hands began to shake uncontrollably.

She did not understand. Not at first. Not fully. But something in her body did. Something deep within her recoiled. She felt a strange tightening in her chest. A heat in her throat.

Two words sprang to her mind—words she had barely heard, words never spoken in her house or by any decent folk, for that matter.

Sodomites. Sodomy.

They were ugly words. Harsh. Biblical. The kind uttered only in courtrooms and rarely in pulpits. But they were the words used at that time to describe men like these. To label their unspeakable acts.

She did not know what else to call it.

And then she knew. It was as if a bolt of lightning had struck her. But it was not lightning but revelation—sudden, searing, and impossible to ignore.

Josef was one of these men. This was why he had never touched her. Never once—let alone with hunger or need. He had married her, but he had not wanted her. Not in the way a natural man wants a woman. But why had he done it? So that no one would suspect his secret? *How could he deceive her like this?*

She thought of the man at the funeral. The one who stood apart. The one who would not meet her eyes. Could he have been Josef's lover?

Her vision blurred. The room tilted.

Elisabetha wanted nothing more than to run from that room, but instead, she steeled herself to sit there for hours.

She forced herself to look at every image. Every line. Every curve. She did not cry or utter a sound. She simply looked, and looked, and looked—until she had memorized every picture and her fingers were numb.

Then she rose, picked up the entire folder, and walked as quietly as she could into the kitchen, where the tile stove was still lit. She knew she must act quickly before the servants were up to begin their day.

She fed each print into the open grate one by one, watching them curl and blacken into ash. She did not look away. She did not want to contemplate even for a moment what might happen if she were ever caught with such images—surely, it was a criminal offense to possess such things. No wonder her husband had concealed them so carefully.

Elisabetha knew she would take this secret to her grave, if it were the last thing she ever did. To speak of such an abomination—even to her parents—was utterly inconceivable.

Chapter Six
Home

The townhouse in Sins was quiet when Elisabetha locked the door for the last time. The brass key felt heavy in her hand, perhaps because she knew she would never use it again. She had sold the property for what the broker called a "respectable sum" and dismissed the servants the day before. Marta had wept. Therese had kissed her hands. Elisabetha thanked them, but no tears came.

She had spent the final night alone, surrounded by boxes and silence. She had only finished packing up the library that evening—each volume wrapped in linen and stacked reverently like sacred relics. She slept in her narrow bed one last time, the house still smelling faintly of ink and dust.

At dawn, the large moving cart arrived.

The hired driver was a quiet man with a thick moustache and a wool cap pulled low over his brow. He loaded the trunks, pieces of furniture, and many wooden crates without comment. Elisabetha climbed in beside him, her black cape pulled tight, her gloves already damp with morning frost.

The journey back to the Aargauer countryside was long and slow. The cart creaked over cobblestones, then gravel, then dirt. The hills rolled past like old memories. She saw the pear trees again—bare now, their branches skeletal against the sky. The smell of woodsmoke and thawing earth filled her lungs. Villages flickered past, each one smaller than the last.

Elisabetha passed the schoolhouse where she had borrowed books from the schoolmaster as a child. The stone bridge where she sat when she first read Goethe's poetry. The field where she had once overheard her father mutter, "*She'll never marry a farmer.*" Each landmark felt like a ghost.

She did not speak.

When the cart finally turned onto the familiar lane, her breath caught. The Villiger farmhouse stood as it always had—stoic, square, and slightly slumped with age. Smoke curled from the chimney. The barns sprawled beside it. The pear tree she used to climb still stood.

Her father was waiting at the gate.

He did not smile, but he nodded once and took her gloved hand in his calloused one. "You're home," he said simply.

Her mother emerged from the kitchen, wiping her hands on her apron. She did not embrace her daughter, but she touched her cheek briefly, as if to confirm that she was real, after an absence of twelve years.

The cart was unloaded. The books were carried into a vacant barn, where her father had cleared space. Elisabetha oversaw the stacking herself, directing the placement of each crate with quiet precision. Her father watched her, arms crossed, saying nothing.

That evening, the family ate together in the big farm kitchen. The tile stove was still lit. The sausages hung from the rafters. A sour trace of vinegar and cabbage hung in the kitchen, rising from the cellar below. Elisabetha sat in her old place, her hands folded in her lap.

Her mother asked simply, "What happened to Josef?"

Elisabetha stirred her leek soup gently with her spoon to make it cool faster. "He died," she said softly.

"Yes, so you said. But you did not say how," Appollonia Villiger responded.

Elisabetha offered nothing further. Her parents exchanged a brief look across the table.

Her father pressed, "And you were never with child? Not even once?"

She shook her head. "No."

They said nothing more. The meal proceeded in silence.

In the days that followed, Elisabetha worked harder than she ever had before. She rose before dawn, helped with the milking, scrubbed the kitchen, stitched linens, churned butter, and learned to make sausages and preserves under her mother's exacting guidance. She did not complain. She did not retreat to the barn to read. She was determined to make herself useful, as she had promised.

Her hands blistered. Her back ached. But her mother began to praise her. Her father began to nod approvingly. The neighbors whispered less.

One afternoon, her mother found her in the barn, sitting on a crate, reading. She didn't scold. She sat beside her daughter and said, "You always did love books more than people."

Elisabetha smiled faintly. "Books never asked me to be someone else."

Her mother said nothing, but she stayed a while.

One evening, as Elisabetha and her mother peeled potatoes by lamplight, her father appeared. After a few minutes of silently puffing away on his pipe, he cleared his throat.

"There's a man we know," he said. "From the Luzernerland. Mathias Stirnimann. A widower. Has a two-year-old boy."

Her mother chimed in. "He's decent. Devout. Hardworking. Not young, but not too old. He's looking for a wife."

Elisabetha lowered her eyes and said nothing.

Her father pressed on. "We let you have it your way the first time, *Tochter*. But you must admit, it didn't work out so well, did it?"

Elisabetha did not deny it.

Her mother added, "You're thirty-nine. And we all know…well…you're not exactly a catch. And you read too much."

Elisabetha's throat tightened. But she did not argue.

Her mother softened. "He's kind. He won't mind the books. You won't be alone forever, Lisbeth. Not if we can help it."

Elisabetha looked down at her hands, rough now from work. She thought of Josef. Of his silence. Of year upon year of his coldness. Of the river.

She nodded once. If this was to be her fate, she would not shrink from it.

"I'll meet him," she said quietly.

Chapter Seven
The Farmer from Ottorüthi

Ottorüthi was a name older than memory. A meadow once cleared by a man named Otto, or so the legends said. The old Swiss German suffix *rüthi* means a clearing, meadow, or place made habitable by labor. But no one in the nearby hamlet of Bertiswil (*BAIR-teess-veel*) gave its origin a second thought. It was simply Ottorüthi—the Stirnimann farm, vast and enduring, tucked into the Luzerner countryside like a stone in the palm of God.

It was not a village, not even a hamlet. It was a farm—but vast enough to feel like a world. The fields stretched in every direction, stitched with hedgerows and low stone walls. Cows moved slowly through the morning mist. Chickens scratched at the dirt. The barn doors groaned like old men.

The Stirnimanns had worked this land for generations. Jakob Stirnimann, Mathias's father, was a man of few words and capable hands. He believed in early hours, straight furrows, and the dignity of silence. Anna Maria Krauer, his wife, kept the house with a stern grace. She boiled linen in lye, churned butter, and baked crackling loaves of bread before dawn. She taught her many strapping sons to pray the rosary and ask God's blessing before lifting the scythe.

Mathias Stirnimann was born there in 1793, the first son of Jakob and Anna Maria. The babe came into the world broad and brown, with enormous hands and feet and eyes the color of cornflowers. By the time he was twelve, he could lift a hay bale without flinching. By the time he was fifteen, Mathias could plow a field in half the time of any hired hand. By the time he was twenty, he was a mountain of a man.

They called him *der Riese von Bertiswil*—the giant of Bertiswil.

He stood a half foot over six feet—just shy of two meters, though no one in Bertiswil measured giants in centimeters. His shoulders filled doorways. His biceps were carved by hard labor. He did not boast. He did not need to. His strength was quiet, like the Reuss in winter—slow, deep, and steady.

He was a *Steinstossen* champion. The traditional sport, practiced since at least the thirteenth century in Alpine communities, meant "stone throwing." It involved lifting and hurling massive stones—

sometimes over eighty kilos—for distance, and was one of Switzerland's oldest strength competitions.

They still spoke of it in the taverns. The day Mathias Stirnimann tossed the heaviest stone anyone had ever attempted to throw.

It had rained the night before, and the field was slick with mud. The stone lay in the center—quarried from the Reuss valley, dark and pitted, near ninety kilos. Men had tried to lift it all morning. Some managed to hoist it a few centimeters off the ground. None threw it.

Then Mathias stepped forward.

He was not exactly young then. Thirty-five, maybe more. Broad in the shoulders. Spare with his words. He rolled up his sleeves, spat once, and gripped the stone with his hands like it owed him something.

He lifted it to his chest. Then overhead.

He threw it.

It landed past the marked line. Past the second stake. Past the place where the butcher had bet his coin.

Needless to say, no one matched it that day. No one matched it in the years to come, either. When he passed through Bertiswil on market days, men nodded respectfully and women whispered. *Der Riese*, they said. The giant. Large. Strong. Quiet.

He could carry a calf across the yard without panting. He could split a log with one swing. He could lift wooden beams that made other men groan.

As the boy grew to be a man, the villagers told stories, spinning him into a legend. How he once pulled an overloaded cart from a ditch with his bare hands. How he stood in the Reuss during spring flash floods and survived. How he saved three people from a burning farmhouse, carrying one on each arm and the last one on his back.

In fact, some said he was carved from the land itself—not born, but quarried.

And when he walked through the pastures, the ground seemed to remember him.

But Mathias Stirnimann was much more than his size or his strength. He did not drink much. Didn't even care to smoke a pipe. He was a man of his word. He was a devout Catholic who prayed the rosary daily and a credit to his parents and his friends. A man of the soil, stone, and silence.

He kept bees. He mended fences. He knew the names of every *Knecht,* every dairy cow, every plant.

He had not yet made a vow. He had not yet buried a wife. Not yet buried a child.

He rose, prayed, worked, and slept, steady as the days themselves.

Chapter Eight
The Swan from Rothenburg

There was a time when Mathias Stirnimann believed he might remain a bachelor his entire life. Somehow, he never met the right woman he wanted to take as his wife. He was nearly forty when all of that changed—in the blink of an eye.

He spotted her at Sunday Mass in Rothenburg, a young woman still in the first blush of youth.

Fräulein Maria Emerenzia Widmer.

From the first moment he laid eyes on her, he could not look away. Her neck was long, elegant, milky white—swan-like. Her eyes were violet blue—not the muddy brown of the farm girls he had grown up with, but something regal, almost otherworldly. The pale hue of her skin was a stark contrast to her head full of dark curls. She moved with grace, and when she bowed her head in prayer, he felt something shift inside him. He knew he would make her his wife.

Their courtship was quiet. Gentle. He brought her apples from Ottorüthi and bunches of *Margueritli* from his meadows. She smiled at him in the churchyard. Her voice was soft. Her hands were small.

They married in the spring.

It was true that she was beautiful and sweet, but she was delicate—a fact that had escaped him before the wedding. She was not made for the soil.

She did not hum or sing when she worked. She moved through the house like someone trying not to wake a sleeping child. Her footsteps were light. Her gestures deliberate. She folded the linens with unnecessary precision.

The ancient farmhouse was not built for someone like her. It was drafty. The floors uneven. The stove smoked when the wind turned. But she made it hers. She placed sprigs of lavender in every room. She kept the table polished. She stitched new curtains and hung them without comment.

Mathias's bride did not complain. Not when the milk soured. Not when the rain came through the roof. Not when the hens stopped laying. She simply took it all in stride. She boiled water. She lit candles. She swept the floor twice. When the wind came through the cracks in the wall, she shivered, but then simply pulled her shawl tighter and went on about her work.

She kept a small mirror wrapped in a linen cloth beneath the bed. Not for vanity. For order. Each morning, she would sit at the edge of the bed and unwrap it as if it were something sacred. She used it to help her part her ebony hair with a bone comb, which she then twisted into a coil and fastened with two pins. One was bent. She used it anyway.

Her bodice was always fastened with care. Not tight. Not loose. Just enough to hold her upright. She wore the same pair of boots every Sunday, polished with tallow and stitched at the heel. Mathias once offered to buy her new ones. She thanked him with a smile but declined his offer.

When she prayed, she closed her eyes. She looked down, lips moving, hands still.

Her husband admired her sometimes from the doorway. She did not know he was there. Or if she did, she did not show it.

During her first pregnancy, Emerenzia, as she was called, had begun to sew in the afternoons, her back braced against the wall, her feet resting on a folded wool blanket. She stitched slowly, with small, even movements, as if the steadiness of her hands might steady the life inside her. She did not speak of the pain in her hips or the way her breath caught when she bent to pick something up.

Mathias brought her favorite apples from the orchard and left them on the table without comment. He had built a cradle from pine and lined it with lambswool. He did not ask what name she had chosen. He did not speak of sons or daughters. But he tripled his daily prayers.

On Saturday evenings, he sat beside her and polished her boots for Sunday morning Mass. He ran his thumb lingeringly along the grain of the leather and said nothing.

She folded the baby's linen shifts and placed them in the chest at the foot of their bed. She lit a candle and whispered a prayer to the *Jungfrau Maria.* Her hands lingered on her belly, not protectively, but as if listening.

The house was quiet. Outside, the wind moved through the grass like a hand through hair.

Mathias hoped for a son who would be his heir. But more than that, he hoped for breath. For warmth. For a cry that did not end in silence.

The first child came during a hard spring. A girl. Emerenzia named her Anna Maria Crescentia Emerenzia Barbara, as if giving her a name worthy of a queen might shield her from harm. The child had fine golden hair and a quiet disposition. She liked to sit in her mother's lap and trace the embroidery on her sleeves. One winter evening, she developed a fever that would not break. The doctor from Rothenburg came twice. The priest came once. By dusk the next day, the child was gone.

The second girl, Anna Maria Barbara Josepha, was born with a strong cry and a full head of dark curls, like her mother. Emerenzia believed she would live. She wrapped her in wool and sang to her in a voice so soft it barely stirred the air. But in her twelfth month, scarlatina swept through Bertiswil. The child's skin flushed deep red. Her breathing grew ragged. She died in her father's arms.

The third daughter, Anna Maria Barbara Sophia, was born in silence. She lived only four days. On the fifth morning of her life, Emerenzia found her cold in her cradle, her tiny hands curled like rose petals.

Each name was a litany. Each death an unhealable wound.

Emerenzia did not wail. She did not tear her hair or curse the heavens. She folded the linens. She lit the candles. She knelt at the foot of the bed and prayed the rosary until she was hoarse.

Mathias buried the children himself, one by one, in the Marienkirche's tiny graveyard in Bertiswil. He carved their names into the wooden crosses with his own hands. Not with flourish. Not with artistry. Just the letters, plain and deep, as if to keep them from being worn away by time and the elements.

The house was especially quiet the night after the third burial. The fire had gone out. The shutters were drawn. The wind moved through the eaves like a voice too tired to speak.

Emerenzia sat at the kitchen table, her hands folded in her lap. She had not lit the lamp. Her face was pale in the dark, her eyes wide and dry. She had not wept this time. Not yet.

Mathias stood in the doorway. He had washed the earth from his hands but not from under his nails. His shirt was still damp from the digging. He did not move toward her at first.

She looked up at him. Not pleading. Not accusing.

He crossed the room and sat beside her. The bench creaked under his tremendous weight. He reached for her hand.

They sat like that for a long time. The stove made soft ticking sounds as it cooled. Somewhere in the rafters, a mouse stirred.

Then, slowly, she leaned against him. Not fully. Just enough to rest her head against his shoulder. Her breath was shallow.

He did not speak. He simply let her lean on him and folded his arms around her.

And when her body began to tremble—not with sobs, but with something quieter, more hollow—he tightened his arms slightly and placed his chin atop her head. They sat like this together and stared into the darkness.

The villagers said that Emerenzia Stirnimann was too fragile for farm life. That she belonged in a parlor, not a pasture. But Mathias never blamed her. He only grew quieter. He rose earlier. He prayed longer.

And when he walked alone, he sometimes went to the tiny church graveyard where the three small crosses lay, weathered by rain and time.

He did not speak to them. He did not kneel.

He simply stood, hat in hand, and let the wind pass through him.

Chapter Nine
The One Who Was Not Taken

Mathias had not touched his wife in months. After the third burial, something inside him had closed. Not out of anger. Not out of blame. But out of fear—a dread so deep it had no name. It clawed at him. He could not bear to plant again what the earth would only plunder.

One night, as they sat beside the stove, he spoke.

"We don't have to," he whispered. "Not again. Ever. Not if it means…"

He did not finish the sentence. He could not say the names. They hung suspended in the air anyway.

Emerenzia looked at him. Her face was pale and pinched in the firelight. Her hands were folded in her lap.

"I will have a child that lives, *min Schatz*," she said. "Or die trying."

He turned away. He did not argue. He knew her voice when it held that kind of final stillness.

And so, in the hush of winter, they lay together again. Because she had chosen to hope, and he had chosen her.

❦

The boy was born in late summer, when the barley was high and the air hung heavy with dust. He came into the world with a cry that shook the rafters—*ein Riesenbaby*, the midwife said, huge like his father. His shoulders were broad. His fists clenched. His lungs strong.

Emerenzia labored for hours. Her breath came in gasps. Her body trembled and poured down cold sweat. The midwife whispered prayers. Mathias stood outside, unmoving, as her screams split the air. He wished the earth would swallow him whole.

When the child was placed in his mother's arms, she smiled. But her hands shook. Her skin was deathly pale. She did not speak.

They named him Kandid (*KAHN-deet*) after Mathias's favorite brother who had died in early childhood—a name that meant purity, light, and perhaps, survival.

He suckled at his mother's breast with force. He grew quickly. His tiny thighs were thick. His grip strong. But Emerenzia seemed to grow weaker with each passing day. Her face thinned. Her voice softened to a mere breathy whisper. She moved through the house like a shadow of herself.

It was as if the boy drained the life out of his mother, bit by bit, with every feeding. She did not complain. She did not ask for rest. She folded the linens. She lit the candles. She whispered the rosary with a voice that barely stirred the air. She rocked Kandid soundlessly at dusk. She had neither the strength to hum nor sing.

One morning, Mathias found his wife standing at the window, holding the boy against her breasts. Her shawl had slipped from her shoulders. The light caught in her hair. She did not turn when he entered. She only smiled and said, "He's so warm."

By the time Kandid turned one, Emerenzia was gone.

Mathias buried her in the family plot in the Marienkirche's cemetery, beside their three daughters. He carved her name into a wooden cross with the same knife he had used for the others. He did not speak. He saved his helpless tears for his pillow at night.

He found her bone comb beneath the bed, wrapped in linen. He held it for a long time, then placed it back without unwrapping it.

He was forty-seven. Now a widower. A father to a boy who had lived when all of his siblings had not.

He could not stop thinking that God was punishing him. For what, he did not know. But it must have been something. This was what he had been taught since he was a small boy, after all.

The days found their rhythm. He rose before dawn. He fed the animals. He turned the soil. He brought Kandid to his sister's house, where the boy would be looked after while Mathias worked. In the early evening, he would pick him up and carry him home on his shoulders.

He did not know how to sing to a child. But he put his son atop his knees and cuddled him in his strong arms. He lit the candles. He folded the linens. He prayed.

Kandid toddled toward the stove one morning, arms outstretched, laughing at the clatter of the kettle. Mathias watched him, unsure whether to smile or cry.

The boy lived. He grew. He laughed sometimes, though Mathias did not know what to do with laughter.

He knew he could not keep this up forever. The child needed a mother. The house needed a woman's warmth.

Eventually, he knew he would have to find a wife. Not for love. Not for comfort. But to rebuild what had been broken. To make a life out of what remained.

Chapter Ten
A Promise Made

Mathias Stirnimann arrived in the hamlet of La Pierraz on horseback one afternoon during the autumn of 1840, the animal lathered and slow from the climb. He had ridden for days from Bertiswil in *Kanton* Luzern, crossing valleys and forested passes, the reins heavy in his hands, as if sorrow itself had weight. He had left Kandid in the capable hands of his sister and the farm in those of his *Leutknecht,* Uli. He told himself he had come for understanding—for quiet, for prayer. But the truth was simpler, and more aching: he came for a miracle.

Not the kind sung about in pulpits. Not thunder or visions. But something smaller. A word that would not bruise. A gaze that would not make him flinch. A sign that life, however scarred, might still be holy.

He was father to one surviving son. The rest—his wife, his baby daughters—lay buried in Bertiswil, beneath wooden crosses he had carved with his own trembling fingers. He carried their names like rosary beads, worn smooth by grief.

He had heard of her—Marguerite Bays, the young seamstress of La Pierraz, near Siviriez in *Kanton* Fribourg. A woman who prayed with a kind of fierce gentleness, who visited the sick and spoke of suffering not as punishment, but as a thread stitched into grace. It was rumored that she carried the wounds of Christ in her flesh, though she never spoke of them. She lived simply, in a small cottage scented with beeswax and thyme, where the poor found warmth and the grieving found solace. People came to her not for spectacle, but for stillness.

Mathias had worked in Fribourg as a young man, hauling timber and stone, mastering the Swiss French *patois* along the way. He was well aware of the way her name was spoken among the people, always with reverence. Now, hollowed by loss, he felt a sudden, inexplicable need to see her.

He had stopped to ask where he might find her home. After riding a short distance through the hamlet and locating the cottage, he dismounted, legs stiff, heart uncertain. He knocked, and the door creaked open. *Der Riese von Bertiswil* had to bend almost double to enter her modest hut.

Inside, Marguerite sat in front of the fire, mending a child's garment, her fingers moving with quiet precision. She didn't look up right away. When she did, her gaze was steady, unafraid, unsurprised. It was almost as if she had been expecting him.

"I've heard that God listens to your prayers," Mathias said, voice rough from the road. "I need someone who understands sorrow."

She gestured to the chair near the hearth. No words. Just a smile of welcome.

He sat, hands clasped like a man holding something fragile. Then he spoke—haltingly—of his wife, of the infant daughters buried at home, of the one son who remained and the weight of surviving. Of the guilt that clung to him like frost. Of the strange longing to marry again, not to replace, but to rebuild.

Marguerite listened without interruption. Then she rose, poured a cup of warm milk from a copper jug on the hearth, and handed it to him. Her voice, when she finally spoke, was low and unhurried, like water over stone. She asked about his home. About his son. About whether he'd slept and eaten.

Then she led Mathias to the small room she used as a chapel and invited him to kneel before a crudely carved wooden figure of *die heilige Maria* which rested upon a simple *Altärli.* An imposing crucifix of black wood hung on the wall behind it. The air was cool, scented with pine and candle smoke. She knelt beside him, her prayers silent. Yet he felt them like a balm on cracked skin, seeping into places he hadn't known were wounded.

"Sorrow," Marguerite said at last, "is not a punishment from God, Mathias. It is a thread. If you stitch it to Christ's own suffering, it will hold."

He asked if she would pray for him—to find a wife, to have children again.

"I will," she said. "But I will also pray that you do not forget the ones you've lost. Let your love for them be the soil where new joy grows."

She produced from her apron pocket a small square of linen, stitched with a cross. "Carry this when you feel alone. Not for luck, but for remembrance. For comfort."

The light that slanted through the small window caught the worn threads of her clothing. Mathias looked at her, eyes wet but clear.

"I want to build something new. But I also want to be worthy of it."

Marguerite nodded slowly. "Then begin with those who have nothing. The widow with no bread. The child with no shoes. The old man who sits alone and forgotten."

She paused for a few moments, her eyes fixed on his. It felt as if her gaze pierced his very soul. "When you serve them, you serve Christ. And when you do it with love, God will not forget."

"Do you think He will bless me again?" he dared to ask.

She smiled—not with certainty, but with peace. "Blessings come in many forms, Mathias. Some arrive as children. Some arrive as strength. Some arrive as the quiet joy of knowing you did some good in this world."

She placed her hand over the folded, stitched linen he now clutched between sweaty fingers. "Let this be your new beginning."

The snow came early to Ottorüthi in the winter of 1841, soft and unrelenting. Mathias Stirnimann stood in the barn, brushing down his horses, lost in thought. He hadn't spoken about his experience in Fribourg to anyone since returning. Not because he had nothing to say, but because the silence had become a kind of prayer.

He thought often of Marguerite Bays's words.

"*If you stitch your sorrow to Christ's own suffering, it will hold.*"

At first, he hadn't really understood her words. He'd imagined a seam, a thread, a garment mended. But now, as he watched his son sleeping by the fire, he began to see.

It meant the grief wouldn't tear him apart.

It meant the sorrow could be carried—not alone, not as punishment, but as part of something sacred. Christ had suffered. And in that suffering, there was room for Mathias's own. Not to erase it, but to hold it.

He began to live differently. Even more quietly, if such a thing were possible. But where once he had lived only for himself and those closest to him, he now looked around for others he might serve. He brought baskets of vegetables from his farm to the widow down the road. He repaired the roof of the church without being asked. He taught his son how to treat animals gently. He gave Emerenzia's shawl to the young, pregnant wife of one of his farmhands.

And when he felt the ache arise—when the memory of his wife's voice or fragmented images of his beautiful baby girls caught him off guard—he reached for the linen square which he stored in the drawer where he kept his wife's rosary, prayerbook, and wedding ring.

Not for luck, but for remembrance. For comfort.

He did not forget them. His longing for them did not stop. But it no longer hollowed him. It held.

The wind pressed against the shutters, and the fire hissed low in the hearth. Mathias sat alone at the wooden farmhouse table in the kitchen.

Kandid was curled on the floor with a wooden cow and a scrap of wool he called "grass." His cheeks flushed pink, his socks mismatched. He looked up when his papa called his name.

"Come here, *Bueb.*"

The toddler climbed into his father's lap, warm and wiggling. Mathias wrapped his arms around him and looked down at the boy.

"Do you know why I gave you your name?" he asked softly.

Kandid shook his head, thumb in his mouth.

"You're named after someone special. My brother. Your uncle. He was a good boy. He didn't get to grow up."

Kandid blinked. "Was he little like me?"

Mathias nodded. "He was, yes. He had a soft voice and strong hands. He used to sing all the time. He was kind."

Kandid leaned his head against his papa's chest. "Is he in heaven with Mama and my sisters?"

"I believe so," Mathias said. "And I think he's glad you carry his name."

The man paused for a few moments before he spoke again. "You don't need to understand it yet," he whispered. "Just know you're part of something good. Something that was not taken."

Kandid yawned, curling deeper into his father's comforting arms.

Outside, the snow whispered against the glass. Inside, Mathias held his son and his sorrow, stitched together by memory and grace.

Yet there was something more. It is true that Mathias Stirnimann was a deeply good and gentle soul. But unbeknownst to everyone—including himself—the deaths of his three baby daughters and his wife in such quick succession had twisted him, quietly and irrevocably.

He became fanatical in his religious devotion. Marguerite Bays had offered him gentle counsel, but he took her words to an extreme she had never intended. In Mathias's mind, if he did not go above and beyond in sacrifice and good works, his son would die. Any future children would die. His future wife, too. He bargained with God—not for blessings, but for protection. He offered the whole of himself, all he owned, in exchange for their safety.

He became a *Friedensrichter*—justice of the peace—walking from farm to farm to hear disputes and settle grievances. The soles of his boots wore thin from the miles. And still, he ran the farm at Ottorüthi, with a *Leutknecht* and other *Knechte* to help, but never to replace him. He would never let go of the land. Not even in grief. Not even in penance.

He believed that if he walked far enough, judged wisely enough, sacrificed deeply enough, God would spare them.

It was not faith.

It was fear, dressed in devotion.

Chapter Eleven
The Auction

The farm auction was held behind a barn in Abtwil, just over *Kanton* Luzern's border into Aargau. Mathias Stirnimann had come to look at a pair of oxen, though he wasn't sure he'd buy. The ground was soft from the previous night's rain, and the air was pungent with the scents of straw, animal dung, and pipe smoke. Men stood in clusters, boots caked with mud, voices low and practical.

He recognized Johann Villiger from Geltwil. He had last seen him at a timber sale a few months before. They nodded to each other, exchanged a few words about the price of rye, the weather, the state of the roads. Villiger was a man of few flourishes—rather squat, blunt, with a voice like grit.

After the auction, *Herr* Villiger invited Mathias to drink a beer with him in a nearby tavern. Inside, the dim warmth and the smell of hops and woodsmoke settled around them. Villiger chose a quiet corner and ordered two beers.

"You're still farming near Bertiswil?" Villiger asked.

Mathias nodded. "I took over the farm at Ottorüthi after my parents died of the grippe."

Herr Villiger's brow furrowed. "You've got a boy, I heard."

Mathias gave a brief nod. "Kandid. He's two."

Villiger pursed his lips. Then he asked quietly, "And your wife?"

Mathias shook his head. "I'm a widower. Lost my wife about a year ago. And three baby daughters in the last few years as well."

Herr Villiger was silent for a moment. He shifted his weight, then puffed on his pipe, the smoke drifting toward the window. Sorrow tightened his brow as he looked away.

"I'm terribly sorry," he said. "That's hard. I lost my twin sons to diphtheria when they were just young *Buebe*. Nearly broke me."

Mathias nodded once, the way men do when words are too small.

Villiger drew even harder on his pipe, the bowl glowing red. Then he cleared his throat. "I've a daughter who is moving back to the farm soon. Elisabetha Moser. She's recently been widowed, too. Thirty-nine. No children. She's humble. Doesn't waste words." He hesitated. "She does like to read, though." *Herr* Villiger added this last bit almost apologetically.

Mathias said nothing.

"She's got means," Villiger added. "Her husband was the town librarian in Sins. Left her a house, a whole library, some money. She's selling the place before coming home to her mother and me."

Now it was Mathias's turn to look out the window. Then he looked back at Villiger. "You're offering her hand?"

"I'm offering a meal," Villiger said with a smile. "*Zmittagässä* some Sunday. You come and meet her mother and we'll talk."

Mathias nodded. After a few moments of silence, he said, "I'll come."

Johann Villiger clapped Mathias once on the shoulder and drained the rest of his stoneware mug.

Mathias watched the foam settle on his own beer.

Yes. He would come.

Chapter Twelve
Courtship

Mathias Stirnimann had ridden from Ottorüthi in Luzern to the Villiger farm outside Geltwil in *Kanton* Aargau, as he had promised.

The farmhouse stood low and broad, its roof heavy with snow, its shutters painted a fading green. The barns leaned slightly westward. A dog barked once and was quiet.

Inside, the kitchen smelled of boiled potatoes, pipe smoke, and starch. The table, scrubbed to a pale sheen, was laid with Appollonia's best homespun linen cloth, and the bench cushions had been beaten and laid flat. A soot-darkened crucifix hung above the tile stove, and a small framed print of the Sacred Heart rested on the windowsill beside a pot of parsley.

Elisabetha was not there—not yet. She was still in Sins, settling the sale of her house. But her name was.

Johann Villiger had spoken first, his voice low and graveled. "Our daughter is a good woman. Quiet. Steady. I won't pretend she's anything like her mother—not a true farm wife by nature. But she'll do what's required of her."

Appollonia Villiger nodded, her hands folded in her lap. "Our Lisbeth is still young enough to begin again," she said, smoothing the tablecloth. "And we'd be glad to see her with someone kind."

Frau Villiger had served boiled parsley potatoes, roasted *Zibele*—onions—and thick slabs of country ham for their midday meal. She poured *Süssmost* into stoneware mugs and sat beside her husband, watching Mathias with a kind of cautious hope.

"She's not looking to be rescued," Elisabetha's mother continued. "But she wouldn't turn away a man who saw her as she is."

Mathias had eaten slowly, listening. He had not yet seen Elisabetha. But he had already begun to imagine the shape of her silence.

They met for the first time in spring.

Several months had passed. Elisabetha had sold the house in Sins, returned home, and begun the slow work of becoming a farm wife. She had learned to milk the cows, to bake bread in the old stone oven, to scrub the floors with vinegar and ash. Her hands had grown rough, her back stronger. She did not complain.

When Mathias arrived, she was not prepared for the sight of him.

She had expected a man of quiet piety, perhaps thin and solemn. But the figure who stepped inside the house was enormous—broad-shouldered, long-limbed, with a ruddy face that startled her. He looked far younger than his years. His nose was large, his mouth wide and generous. His ears protruded a fair bit, giving him a slightly boyish air. His light brown hair refused to be tamed, curling at the edges like a child's. His large, cornflower blue eyes held no guile. Although he had a friendly face, it could never be called handsome. But he was large and solid. Somehow, the sheer mass of him made her feel safe.

Elisabetha did not understand her sudden attraction to the man. But it was undeniable. *His hands must be nine inches long*, she thought absently. For a moment, she imagined those hands stroking her back. Because somehow she knew this giant of a man would be gentle.

Their courtship was unhurried. He came on Sundays, sometimes on Wednesdays. He rode his horse all the way from Ottorüthi in *Kanton* Luzern each time. They walked the fields, spoke of crops and Scripture, sat beneath the pear tree when the weather was fine. He brought her bunches of wildflowers. He asked about her reading. She asked about his son and the daughters and wife he had lost. Once she had traveled to Ottorüthi with her parents in their horse cart to meet Kandid. She was enamored of the boy the first time she saw him—he was sweet, quiet, and the image of his father, only with a mop of black curls. One time Mathias had brought her a small volume of German love poetry with a heart wreathed in red roses on the cover. There could be no better way to her heart, Elisabetha thought. Finally, he dared to hold her hand.

One afternoon, she spoke plainly.

"I know I'm far from a beauty," she said quietly. She kept her eyes on her hands. "And I won't be a model farm wife. But I've made progress. I can cook, and I can bake and make sausage, and I won't mind the work."

Mathias nodded, listening.

"I'd like to keep my library," she added. "I love to read. I know that's not usual."

He smiled softly and shook his head. His blue eyes twinkled. "I don't mind any of that."

What Mathias seemed most interested in was her faith. He asked if she prayed the rosary daily, if she attended Mass, if she would raise their children to be faithful. She answered yes, without hesitation.

But before he asked her to marry him, he laid down his requirements.

"I need your solemn promise," he said, "that you will treat Kandid as your own child. And that you will support me—fully—in my vow to serve God to the utmost of my ability. These sacrifices will affect your life and the lives of our children."

He did not elaborate any further.

He told her that his work as *Friedensrichter* would take him from home often. Outside of that, there was still the farm to run. She would be alone with the children, and perhaps a servant or two, for long periods of time, and she must be willing to accept this.

Elisabetha nodded. She had lived through far worse. Her first husband had almost never been home—had almost never even spoken to her for twelve long years. He had never loved or even liked her. She herself hadn't felt any love for Josef Moser for many years, although she would never breathe a word of this to anyone.

This—this was different.

She looked at Mathias then, directly.

Elisabetha felt pride in his work. He was an intelligent farmer, schooled enough to read French and Latin, and he even understood the Swiss legal code. He spoke plainly, but with precision. He did not senselessly flatter her. He did not hide from the truth.

"There's something else I must say," she said. "I may be too old to bear children. I don't want to lead you on, only to see you disappointed or angry with me."

Mathias did not flinch. He folded his hands and nodded once.

"That is in God's hands," he said. "Not our own. His will be done."

Elisabetha felt content with this.

A strange mixture of peace and trembling moved through her, as though something vast had shifted. She did not yet understand the weight of the life she was choosing. She knew only that she would walk toward it and leave the past behind forever.

Chapter Thirteen
The Wedding

The proposal had been simple. No kneeling, no declarations. Just a quiet moment in the orchard behind the Villiger farmhouse, where Mathias had asked if she would come to Ottorüthi as his wife. Elisabetha had nodded, her hands still dusted with flour from the morning's baking. It was enough.

They married in September, in the chapel at Muri Abbey near Geltwil. She had been baptized in that chapel. Aargau was her home canton, and it felt right for the ceremony to be there. The Villigers rode together in the horse cart, meeting Mathias at the chapel steps. The bride wore her Aargauer *Tracht*, the starched cap tied securely beneath her chin. She carried a small bouquet of asters, their purple petals trembling in the stiff breeze. Mathias wore a navy blue suit.

The ceremony lasted only minutes. When Elisabetha turned to her parents, she saw tears brimming in their eyes—not the tight-lipped, dry-eyed sorrow they had worn on their faces at her first wedding in Sins, but something altogether different. Something like joy. This made her smile.

After the ceremony, they returned to the Villiger farmhouse for a wedding breakfast that Appollonia and Elisabetha had begun preparing two days earlier. The table was laid with a heavy, hand-spun linen cloth, embroidered at the edges with white thread. Aster blossoms and *Margueritli*, cut fresh that morning, were tucked into a pewter pitcher at the center. The windows were open to the September light.

There were several enormous, glistening *Zöpfe*, still warm from the oven, their golden crusts brushed with egg. Appollonia had made *Birrewegge*—a rolled pastry filled with dried pears, nuts, and a whisper of *Kirsch*—and Elisabetha had insisted on baking *Rahmwähe*, the creamy custard tart she remembered so fondly from her childhood. A wheel of hard *Sbrinz* cheese sat beside a crock of fresh butter, flanked by thick slices of *Emmentaler* and a wedge of *Tilsiter* wrapped in waxed cloth. Appollonia had also brought out a small round of goat cheese from the cellar, its rind dusted with ash and thyme. The cheeses were arranged with care, each one a quiet tribute to the land that produced them. Pots of fruit preserves and platters of hard-boiled eggs, pickled beets, and slices of smoked ham from the cellar rounded out the fine spread.

They drank coffee with thick cream and clinked glasses of *Suser*, the young, fizzy wine of early autumn. It was a splendid feast—the kind of table that spoke of women's care and quiet joy.

It was then that Mathias presented his bride with a wedding gift: a gold cross on a thick red-gold chain. The pendant was nearly two inches long, ornate and heavy. On one side, the letters IHS were inlaid—a Latin abbreviation for Jesus. On the reverse was a diamond pattern formed by onyx and mother-of-pearl. Elisabetha held it in her palm, tracing the edges with her thumb. She did not say much, but she knew: this was an heirloom. It would outlast them both.

Later, Mathias and *Herr* Villiger packed Elisabetha's trunks into the cart. The crates of books, household goods, and furniture from Sins would be collected at a later date by several farmhands from Ottorüthi.

Before climbing into the cart, Mathias turned to his new bride's parents and shook their hands with quiet warmth. "This is not goodbye," he told them. "Surely we will be together for Christmas."

Elisabetha looked at her husband with surprise—and something akin to gratitude. Josef had never permitted her to travel home to visit her parents. Not once in twelve years.

Appollonia stepped forward and pressed a small linen-wrapped parcel into her daughter's hands. "For your new home," she said. "It's a good reminder for us all." Elisabetha held the package reverently in her hands. She would unwrap it later, when she had a quiet moment.

She stood for a moment at the gate and said goodbye to both her parents before her husband helped her into the wagon. The farmhouse slipped away behind her. She did not cry, though tears sprang to her eyes. When she turned, her childhood home was already a small dot in the distance.

The asters and daisies in the pitcher would still be fresh tomorrow. The cross lay warm against her chest. A thin ache opened in her, part sorrow, part hope. She did not look back again.

Chapter Fourteen
A New Home

The journey to Luzern took nearly four hours. The newlyweds left just after the wedding breakfast and followed the winding road south through the hills. The cart moved at a steady pace, pulled by a single draft horse, its hooves muffled by the damp earth. The road was uneven in places—rutted from summer rains, edged with moss and fallen leaves. They passed through patches of forest, where the light dappled the path, and then out again into open fields, where the wind carried the scent of cut hay and distant woodsmoke. The cart wheels creaked over gravel and damp earth, and the fields passed in long, slow stretches of green and gold. Elisabetha sat beside Mathias, her hands folded over the linen-wrapped parcel her mother had pressed into them.

They did not speak much. There was no need.

At one point, Mathias said, "I told Kandid I would be bringing his new mama to him today. He's very excited."

Elisabetha turned to him, startled. "You told him?"

He nodded. "He's been under my sister's care. But he knows. He's ready."

She looked down at her hands. She had never held a child—not even once.

They crossed the cantonal border in the early afternoon. The fields grew wider, the trees more sparse. Luzern's soil was darker, richer. The road curved past a small inn, then dropped slightly before rising again toward the Stirnimann land.

She had held the linen-wrapped parcel in her lap for the entire journey. Her fingers traced its edges again and again, feeling the softness of the cloth, the faint shift of something solid wrapped within it.

She waited until they passed the tiny Catholic church in Bertiswil. The road then dipped into a shallow valley, and the wind picked up. Mathias was quiet beside her, his eyes on the horizon.

Elisabetha unwrapped the parcel, unfolding the fabric carefully.

Inside was a small wooden frame. The embroidery was simple but precise—her mother's hand unmistakable. A border of stitched roses and forget-me-nots surrounded a passage from Paul's letter to the Corinthians:

Love is patient. Love is kind.

It is neither proud nor self-seeking.

It keeps no record of wrongs and rejoices in the truth.

It bears all things, believes all things, hopes all things, endures all things.

Love never fails.

The thread was a soft blue, the color of her mother's apron. The cloth smelled faintly of lavender and woodsmoke.

Elisabetha stared at the letters. They were uneven in places, some stitched backwards, others cramped and trembling. Appollonia Villiger had copied them from the family Bible, letter by letter, sounding them out under her breath. It must have taken her weeks. Maybe months.

Beneath the frame was a note, written in her mother's careful hand:

Für deine neue Stube. Du bist nicht allein.

Elisabetha folded the cloth back around the frame and the note, cradling the bundle to her chest. She did not cry. But she felt something she could not identify grip her chest.

She did not speak of it to Mathias. She would hang it later. Not as decoration, but as a tether.

They arrived in the late afternoon. The sun was low, casting long shadows across the fields. Ottorüthi was much larger than she remembered—not just the house, but the land itself. The fields went on forever, stitched with rows of barley and potatoes, bordered by hedgerows and fruit trees. The house, also called Ottorüthi, stood tall and broad, its stone walls weathered and strong.

As the cart pulled in, the farmhands were already waiting. The *Knechte* stood in a line beside the lone milkmaid, their caps doffed, their weatherbeaten faces solemn. Elisabetha stepped down from the cart and nodded to each of them. She did not know what to say, but they bowed their heads respectfully just the same.

Kandid was waiting at the gate with his aunt, his small, chubby hands gripping the slats. He had his father's cornflower blue eyes and a tumble of black curls that caught the light. When Mathias lifted him into his arms and said, "Kandid, this is your new mama," the boy simply looked at her, solemn and curious. Then he reached out his little arms for her. Elisabetha's heart melted. She had never experienced such a feeling.

Inside, the house smelled of wood polish and fresh bread. The rooms were small and plainly kept, the floors swept to a dull shine, the windows washed until the light lay clean across the kitchen table. The air was warm, close, unfamiliar. She stepped over the threshold with the framed linen pressed against her chest, the stitched words resting beneath her fingers. She did not yet know what kind of life awaited her in these rooms. She only knew she was carrying her mother's blessing into it.

That evening after supper, after the trunks were carried in and the house had quieted, Elisabetha found herself sitting in the rocking chair beside her stepson's bed. She had unpacked one of the few books she had brought on the journey—a worn volume of fables with colorful pictures—and Kandid had climbed into her lap without hesitation. She read him the story that belonged to the illustration he liked most, and then she rocked him to sleep in her arms.

It surprised her, how natural it felt—the holding, the warmth, the simple fact of being needed. And in that instant she knew: Kandid was her son, as surely as if he had been born from her own body. She would think of him as such until her dying day.

Mathias stood in the doorway for a moment, watching. He did not speak. But when she looked up, he gave her a small smile—one of thanks, and something more.

Chapter Fifteen
The Wedding Night

Elisabetha sat at the dressing table in her nightgown, brushing her hair. One hundred strokes. Then another hundred. And another. The candlelight flickered against the mirror, casting soft shadows across her face. Her hand moved steadily, but her heart was not calm.

She had not told Mathias. Not about Josef. Not about the years of silence. Not about the fact that she had never been touched by a man—not truly. She was nearly forty, and still a virgin.

Her body embarrassed her. She knew its awkward shape too well: bony legs, thick waist, paunchy belly, flat hips, broad shoulders. A bosom too ample for her short neck. Her face, wide and pale, with gray-blue eyes behind the wire-rimmed spectacles she had worn since she was ten.

The mattress was enormous—longer than any she had ever seen. She noticed it when Mathias entered and quietly got into bed. She knew it must have been custom made to accommodate his tremendous height, and he looked almost regal lying there, his head propped against the pillow, his hands folded across his chest.

Elisabetha kept brushing. The strokes were slower now, deliberate. Her heart beat furiously. She could feel the heat rising in her cheeks, and she knew she was blushing beet red.

Mathias waited a long time before speaking.

"Would you come and lie down beside me?" he asked softly, patting the mattress beside him.

She hesitated. Then, with a breath she did not realize she was holding, she set the brush down. Her feet moved of their own accord, carrying her to the bed. She climbed in beside him, wearing her long nightgown—high-necked, long-sleeved, buttoned at the wrists. It was the same one she had worn every autumn and winter for years. She had not thought to get something else for her wedding night.

Her husband removed her spectacles and placed them gently on the bedside table. Then he blew out the candle.

Mathias did not touch her at first. He simply lay beside her, his breath steady, his presence warm. Then, slowly, he reached for her hand beneath the covers. She let him take it.

When he leaned in to kiss her, she turned her face toward him. His lips were soft, his face smooth, almost as if he had shaved again before coming to bed.

He kissed her again, slower this time, and she felt something shift inside her—a loosening.

Then his fingers found the buttons at her collar. He paused.

She gave the smallest nod. He unfastened them one by one, with care. The fabric parted at her throat, then lower. She felt the cool air on her skin, the heat rising beneath it. Her heart beat so loudly she was sure he could hear it.

He did not rush. He did not pull or fumble. He peeled the gown away like a ribbon from a parcel—slowly, reverently, as if unwrapping something precious.

When he touched her bare shoulder, she flinched. Not from fear, but from the shock of being seen.

"*Du bisch äbe schön*," he whispered.

She blushed harder. She did not believe him. But she let him go on.

In the dark, he pulled her soft body into his hard one. His enormous hands were warm and steady. He ran his fingers through her long brown hair, smoothing it away from her face. She did not utter a sound. She could not.

But Mathias was sweet and gentle. He did not ask questions. He simply held her, touched her with care, and let her feel what it was like to be desired.

It surprised her, how natural it felt. Not just the act itself, but the closeness. The warmth. The way her body responded to him, not with fear, but with something like longing.

She had expected pain. Shame. Awkwardness. But instead, there was a slow unfolding—a quiet heat that rose between them, a rhythm that felt less like surrender and more like arrival.

He kissed her neck, her shoulders, the curve of her full breasts. His touch was almost reverent. She felt herself soften, open, become.

She made no sound, but her body answered him. Her hands found his back, his chest, the line of his jaw. She ran her fingers through his soft light brown hair and caressed his strong arms and muscular shoulders. She traced him like a map she had never been allowed to read until now.

When it was over, she lay with her head on his chest, listening to the rhythm of his breathing. He tucked the blanket around her without a word, his hand resting lightly on her hip.

She felt no shame. Only a quiet astonishment.

She could not have imagined doing this with Josef. Not even once.

Outside, the wind stirred the trees. Her nightgown lay forgotten on the floorboards.

It was a new world.

Chapter Sixteen
The First Morning

Elisabetha woke before the light. The room was cold, the air still. Mathias was already up—she heard the creak of the floorboards, the soft murmur of his voice. When she stepped into the hallway, she saw him standing by the window, rosary in hand, lips moving silently.

He turned when he saw her and smiled.

"Will you pray with me?"

She hesitated. She had not prayed the rosary in some time—not since the Catholic pastor in Sins had denied her husband a burial. But she nodded and stepped beside him. He handed her the rosary.

They prayed together quietly, bead by bead. His voice was low and steady. Hers was barely audible. But they continued together.

Afterwards, he kissed her forehead and they both went to dress. But first, she lingered a moment longer, holding the final bead between her fingers.

In the kitchen, Elisabetha searched for flour to bake bread. The bins were nearly empty. A handful of rye, a scoop of barley. No wheat. Only a small cake of yeast. She frowned, then set to work. She boiled water, ground what she could, mixed and kneaded and shaped. The dough was coarse, but it would rise enough to feed them.

She woke Kandid gently, brushing the hair from his forehead. He blinked at her, confused, a question in his round blue eyes.

"*Wo isch mini Tanti?*"

"She went home," Elisabetha said. "It's just us now."

She dressed him slowly, buttoning his shirt and pants, pulling on his socks, tying his shoes. He clung to her skirt as she moved through the kitchen, watching her with solemn eyes. She gave him two slices of apple and a half cup of milk. He ate quietly.

Mathias returned, dressed for church. He sat at the table and accepted the bread she had baked—rough, dense, but warm. He said a blessing prayer over the meager breakfast. They ate in silence, the three of them. A family, if not yet familiar.

It was Sunday, and they walked to Bertiswil for morning Mass. Mathias carried his young son on his shoulders. The Marienkirche stood at the edge of the village. The church had a *Chääsbissen Turm,* which Elisabetha pointed out to Kandid. "See how it looks just like someone has taken a bite out of a piece of cheese?" He giggled at this.

Inside, the pews were full. Elisabetha felt the eyes of the villagers on her—curious, measuring. Her cheeks flushed scarlet.

She and Mathias sat with Kandid between them. The priest spoke of the misery of purgatory or something or other. She heard only fragments. Her mind was elsewhere—on the bread, on the rosary, on the way the women stared at her dress.

After the service, Mathias introduced her to a few neighbors. She smiled, nodded, forgot every name. A woman with a red scarf. A man with a limp. A child who stared at her shoes.

On the walk home, she thought about *Zmittagässä.* The larder in the farmhouse kitchen was nearly bare. She would need to make do.

"I'm not sure what I can prepare," she said quietly.

Mathias stopped beside the barn and lifted a basket from the ground. It was full of carrots—bright, earthy, freshly pulled.

“We always have an overabundance of carrots,” he said, smiling bashfully. “Can you cook us something with these?”

She looked at the basket, then at him. She nodded.

“Yes,” she said. “I can.”

She did not know then how many ways she would learn to cook carrots. Every recipe her mother had taught her. Every new dish she would invent. Soups, stews, fritters, cakes. Boiled, roasted, steamed, mashed, pickled. Carrots in milk. Carrots with vinegar. Carrots with nothing at all. She would feed this family with carrots until she was given something else.

But for now, she carried the basket into the house, and set it on the table with a sigh.

Chapter Seventeen
The Secret

Elisabetha was surprised by her husband's gentle affection, so unlike Josef's coldness. Mathias touched her with eager desire, spoke to her with patience, kissed her as though she mattered. She had not expected tenderness. It felt like what she imagined love must feel like.

But the secret about her first marriage pressed against her chest like a stone. She had vowed to herself that she would never speak of Josef's truth. At the time she made the vow, she had no idea just how difficult silence would be. She thought it would be simple, that forgetting would come with time. Instead, the secret grew heavier with each passing day, pressing down upon her heart as if it might crush her.

She thought of it at the strangest times. In church, when the priest spoke of truth and confession, her mind wandered to Josef. She remembered the way he avoided her eyes and her touch, the way he refused to speak to her. She remembered the cold loneliness of her bed, the ache of being unwanted. Only after she swore she would take the truth of his secret to her grave did she understand that silence was not an ending but a companion she would carry into every room of her life.

Rocking Kandid every evening, she felt the weight of it more sharply. His small body was warm against hers, his childish breath sweet. She thought of the life she was building now, the family she was trying to shape. And yet Josef's shadow lay between them, a ghost she could not banish.

Despite his kindness, she knew that her deeply religious second husband would never understand. *She* did not understand it herself—not fully. But instinct told her that if Mathias ever learned of it, he would be angry with her—and this she did not deserve. She was a victim of her first husband's deception herself.

Even in bed, when Mathias's breath warmed her neck, the thought intruded. She would turn her face to him, receive his kiss, feel his hand on her shoulder—and then, suddenly, she would remember Josef. The contrast was unbearable. Mathias's tenderness only sharpened her guilt. She loved him—with loyalty, with devotion, with gratitude for his constant affection. But she still had to figure out how to go on living peaceably while Josef's secret remained locked inside her.

Mathias and Elisabetha prayed the rosary together each morning. Bead by bead, prayer by prayer, she whispered the words. But her heart was not free. Each prayer was overshadowed by this burden she carried. Elisabetha wondered if Mathias sensed her unease—the way her voice faltered, the way her eyes dropped to the floor.

She tried to busy herself with household tasks. She scrubbed the floors, mended shirts, baked bread from the meager grain she was given. But even then, the secret intruded. She would be kneading dough, her hands sticky with flour, and suddenly she would think about the pictures Josef had concealed in the next-to-last drawer of the *Biedermeier* desk in his library.

At night, when Mathias slept beside her, she sometimes whispered into the dark: *I must take it to my grave.* Her words were steady, but her hands trembled. She pressed her palms together, as though in prayer, but no prayer came. Only silence.

The secret must remain hers and hers alone.

Chapter Eighteen
The House Without Bread

Elisabetha noticed it at first as an emptiness. The kitchen was not alive in the way a farm kitchen should be—there was no warm scent of rising dough, no steam lifting from pots, no bulging grain bins filled to the brim. There were only a few scoops of rye flour at the bottom of a crock, the hollow feel of the barley jar in her hands, and a small basket of carrots sitting alone on the table like something forgotten.

She tried to reason with herself: perhaps the season, perhaps a temporary shortage, perhaps she had not yet learned Ottorüthi's rhythm. But each morning confirmed it. No wheels of cheese. No slabs of cured meats. No sack of flour hefted into the corner by a sweating *Knecht.* She kept lifting lids and finding air.

She remembered her mother's kitchen, the regular arrival of abundance—frothy milk pails beaded with cold, baskets of apples breathing sweetness, trays of freshly-butchered pork, grain scratching like river sand as it poured into bins. The only items Mama ever had to purchase were things the farm did not produce: sugar, salt, baking powder, spices.

Uli *der Leutknecht* generally came just after dawn with his delivery. The thought occurred to Elisabetha that perhaps he was hoping she would still be asleep when he brought the meager allotted supplies to the farm kitchen. He set a folded cloth on the table and unwrapped it: a handful of grain, a heel of cheese, three eggs, an onion, a small bottle filled with milk. And then finally, the large basket of carrots. He did it quickly, eyes down, as if speed could make the smallness seem larger. Elisabetha thanked him quietly each day, because gratitude had been drilled into her from birth. But the words felt brittle on her tongue.

She began to count, quietly, the way her mother counted stitches. How many slices would the cheese yield if she cut it very thinly? How many mornings would the rye stretch if mixed with barley? She reserved the milk exclusively for her son. Kandid always ate first. Mathias ate second. She ate last, as she had always been taught, but now obedience pressed too hard against necessity.

After only a week, she could not keep her questions folded inside any longer.

"Uli," she asked meekly, when he placed the cloth on the table, "why is there so little for us?"

He paused, fingers still at the knot—a neat square knot he untied the same way every day. He did not look at her. "These are the master's orders."

She let the words sit between them, as if they might thicken into an explanation. They did not. She tried again, gentler, measured.

"But Uli, the fields are full. I see the wagons. The barns are far from empty. Where does it all go?"

Uli's homely face colored, a slow tide that stained his cheeks a dark red. He glanced up, then away, found the knot again and worried it, though it was already loose. "These…are the master's orders." Elisabetha held his gaze, even though he would not return it. She was not a woman who pressed, but that was all about to change.

"I need to understand," she said, more firmly this time. "Uli, I *must* understand what is going on."

He swallowed. The room now carried the scents of onion and cold ash. Outside, a cart rolled past, iron rim humming against hard earth. Uli lifted the cloth, set the basket of carrots straight though they did not need straightening. He opened his mouth, closed it. The blush deepened.

"Uli," she pleaded with a soft urgency, "*please.*"

A small sound came from him, like a boot easing free of mud. He shook his head, not in refusal but in apology, and tugged the knot tight as if that could end the matter. "I… I cannot say."

She felt the answer as clearly as if he had spoken it: this was not an accident of season, nor a temporary miscalculation, but a rule. A choice. A shape pressed onto the household by its master.

"*Danke,*" she said quietly, because the conversation had nowhere else to go. Uli nodded, almost a bow, and slunk away quickly. The door closed behind him with a wooden sigh.

Elisabetha stood a long time with her hands on the table, feeling the grain of the wood under her palms. She tried to think of it as an exercise, a test of skill—how to feed a family every day with such a meager array of foods. She rinsed the carrots, scraped their skins with the dull edge of a knife, set the heel of cheese aside to grate. The onion's bite brought tears, which she welcomed, for they masked the ones born of frustration.

At supper, Kandid finished what was in his small wooden bowl and looked at her with the puzzled patience of a child who trusts the world to be sufficient. She touched his dark curls and told him there would be more in the morning. Mathias ate quietly, his thanks offered without remark on quantity or taste. The silence at the table widened like a crack in winter clay.

That night, Elisabetha lay awake listening to the house breathe: rafters settling, wind threading the gaps, cattle shifting in the barn. The kitchen's bare shelves rose in her mind like a ledger she could not balance. She thought of her mother's hands, always busy, always sure, and of her own, steady but now tasked with spareness.

She did not yet know the reason, but she knew this: this household had been forced to live without bread, and she would somehow have to learn how to make hunger gentle—at least for her son.

Chapter Nineteen
The Line at the Barn

Uli finally broke.

For days he had brought her the same meager offerings—a handful of grain, an onion, a couple of eggs, a small piece of cheese, and the ever-present large basket of carrots. Each time she pressed him, he repeated the same words: "These are the master's orders." But Elisabetha remained persistent, her voice steady, her eyes unyielding. Hunger is a question that will not be silenced.

At last, his face flushed, his hands restless at the knot of the cloth. He muttered, almost inaudibly, "*Bauer* Stirnimann gives generously to the poor."

The words struck her like a blow. She remembered Mathias's solemn request before their marriage—that she promise to support him fully in doing God's will. She had agreed, not knowing exactly what he meant. Now she understood. It meant her own family would live without bread so that strangers might eat.

And yet, even as the truth settled in her chest, Elisabetha felt something unexpected: loyalty. Devotion. She had never felt such things for Josef. With him, there had been only silence, distance, shame. With Mathias, she shared tenderness, intimacy—a physical closeness she had not thought possible. Perhaps it was that intimacy which bound her now, even as she faced his unusual, indefensible choices.

For reasons she did not herself understand, she felt the need to justify her husband, to defend him, though logic told her otherwise. She thought of the words from Saint Paul her mother had embroidered onto linen: *Love is patient. Love is kind. Love endures all things. Love never fails.*

Later that week, Uli came to her in silence. He gestured for her to follow, his eyes lowered, his mouth tight. Elisabetha wiped her hands on her apron and stepped outside. The air was sharp with winter, the ground hard beneath her shoes. Uli led her toward the barns, then stopped short and pointed.

She saw them: a long line of poor, ragged people stretching across the yard. Men with hollow cheeks, women clutching infants, children thinly clad in the frost. Where had they all come from? They waited patiently, eyes fixed on the barn doors. Two of

Mathias's most trusted *Knechte* stood inside, doling out baskets of food—bread, milk, vegetables, cheese, eggs, sausage—to each person and family in turn. The line moved slowly, each basket a small salvation to its recipients.

Elisabetha's breath caught. In that moment, it had all become crystal clear: Ottorüthi's abundance was not for her, not for Mathias, not even for their son. It was for *them*—the nameless poor who came each day to be fed. Her own family was to go hungry for these strangers.

That evening, Kandid whimpered after supper, his small bowl scraped clean. Elisabetha gave him part of her own portion, watching him eat with desperate hunger. Mathias sat in silence, his face calm, as though such sacrifice were natural. How could he bear the sight of his own child's hunger, when the means to ease it lay in his hands?

Elisabetha lowered her eyes to her empty bowl. She thought of Josef, who had never touched her with tenderness, and of Mathias, who had. She thought of the vows she had made, and of the strange devotion that bound her now. She thought about the fact that she had never known hunger in her life until now. And she wondered how long she could defend what her heart told her was indefensible.

Chapter Twenty
The Betrayal

Saturday morning carried its usual hum from Bertiswil—the creak of wagons, the calls of vendors, the chatter of women gathering near the stalls. Market day. Elisabetha knew what it meant: bread, cheese, sausages, milk—abundance laid out in plain sight. And she knew what it would mean if she went.

To go would be a betrayal. Mathias had asked her to support him in doing God's will to the fullest possible extent, and she had promised to obey her husband with her whole heart. Yet Kandid's hunger gnawed at Elisabetha more fiercely than any vow.

She thought of Josef, her first husband, and the tidy sum he had left behind. She thought of the townhouse in Sins, sold after his death, the small chest of gold *Dukaten* she had received and tucked away. Of course, she had told Mathias about her inheritance before their marriage. He had waved it off—told her she could keep it, that he wanted none of it. And now she wondered: was it not meant for this? To feed them when her husband left his family wanting?

But the thought gave her pause. For she knew that it would give Mathias pain to know that his wife had not only betrayed him, but gone behind his back.

Elisabetha considered the way she wracked her brains every day for another way to cook carrots, or *Rüebli*, as they were called in Swiss German. There was *Rüeblisuppe*, stewed carrots, carrots cooked with onion—without the bacon, of course—*Rüeblichüechli*, *Rüebliwähe*, grated carrot salad, baked carrot sticks, steamed carrots. *Rüeblitorte* and *Rüeblipudding* never made an appearance on the farmhouse table; she had no sugar, no honey for such delicacies. It was these thoughts that finally made her decide to go.

She rose, tied on a shawl and bonnet, and took her small coin purse with her. The leather was worn, and the coins inside felt as if they weighed a ton. She held it a moment, trembling. Then she slipped it into her apron pocket and lifted her basket.

The market was alive with noise and color. Farmers called out their wares, women judged freshness with practiced eyes and noses, children darted between stalls. The fragrance of freshly baked breads and cheeses hung thickly in the air. Elisabetha moved quietly, her eyes lowered, her basket close against her hip.

At the bakery stall, the baker's wife stood behind a table, her voice brisk as she served her customers. When it was her turn, Elisabetha pointed to the bread loaves and the tray of crescent rolls. "A loaf of rye. And a dozen *Gipfeli*," she spoke softly.

The baker's wife looked at her with surprise, her sharp tone carrying across the stall. "A dozen? *For the mistress of Ottorüthi?*"

Elisabetha's cheeks burned. She lowered her eyes, laid down her coins, and waited while the rye loaf and rolls were wrapped.

Behind her, she could hear whispers. "Strange, isn't it? *Bauer* Stirnimann feeds beggars from three cantons, yet his wife must buy food at the farmers' market," one of them said.

"Charity should begin at home," another one tsked.

"Buying bread with whose coins, I wonder?" a third murmured. "Not the master's, that's certain."

Elisabetha gathered her purchases without a word. Silence was her shield, the only answer permitted. She turned away, stowing the paper-wrapped *Gipfeli* into her basket as though they were contraband, her face hot with shame.

At the butcher's stall, she asked for sausages and bacon. The butcher's wife just raised her eyebrows but said nothing. She didn't have to—her astonishment was written all over her face. She wrapped the links and the slab quickly in waxed butcher paper. Elisabetha once again set down her coins and moved on.

At the *Chääshändler*'s stall, two women elbowed each other as she approached. "*Look at her—Stirnimann's wife*," one whispered.

"Isn't it shameful? Having to buy food, because her husband gives it all away! And him, owning the most prosperous farm in the Luzernerland! What is *wrong* with that man?"

Elisabetha's hands shook as she pointed to a wedge of cheese. "This one," she said. The cheesemaker's wife weighed it, wrapped it, and handed it to her with lowered eyes and a tight smile. She thanked Elisabetha politely when she handed over her coins.

The mistress of Ottorüthi also bought a liter of milk, a dozen eggs, a slab of butter, and six *Erdöpfel* before she was done. She wanted only to be gone from that place.

On the walk back to the farm, Elisabetha's basket was heavy, but her heart was heavier. Relief surged—

Kandid would eat—he would get more than carrots and grain. But dread pressed against it. She had betrayed her husband's trust. She had broken her promise.

At the threshold she paused, listening for footsteps. The house was quiet. She stole down the narrow steps into the cellar, where the air was cool and smelled of must and damp stone. She placed the cheese and eggs into an empty crock, deposited the bread and rolls into a covered basket, and put the sausages and bacon into an empty wooden box she found. The milk bottle and potatoes she stored inside an old cabinet. Each hiding place felt like a lie, each concealment a wound.

Later, when she was certain that Mathias was far from home, she went down to the cellar with an empty plate and brought it back filled. Kandid sat at the table, his cornflower blue eyes wide, his hands folded before him as if in prayer. Elisabetha cut a slice of bread—thin but generous compared to what he was used to—spread it with butter, topped it with cheese, and placed it in front of him. She poured the fresh milk into a cup and set it beside the plate.

"Eat quickly, *Chind,*" she whispered. "Before your father returns."

The boy obeyed, biting into the *Chääsbrot* with a hunger so fierce it made her ache. She watched him chew, crumbs clinging to his soft baby lips, and felt once again the familiar relief and dread. Each bite was nourishment for her son, but each bite he took reminded her of her sins.

By the time Mathias entered, the plate had disappeared. Only their ordinary, meager dinner remained—stewed carrots, thin broth. Kandid ate quietly, while Elisabetha kept her eyes lowered, her cheeks burning. Mathias bowed his head in prayer, unaware of the secret meal that had passed in his absence.

That night, Elisabetha lay awake beside her husband, clutching the memory of her first trip to the market, her cheeks still flaming. She had fed her child. But the price was betrayal and deceit. She could not tell which burden would prove the greater in the days ahead.

Yet beneath her shame, another thought stirred—a single remark tossed out by one of the gossips at the market: *What is wrong with that man?* Elisabetha had brushed it aside at the time. Now, in the darkness, the words returned with a different weight.

What had those women seen that she had not? And why did the question trouble her more than her own deceit?

Chapter Twenty-One
The Thief of Ottorüthi

Elisabetha carried two burdens now, and both were heavy. Josef's secret lay within her like a stone—a heavier legacy than the books and the money he left behind. And now Mathias's extreme charity, his certainty that pleasing God required complete, total, and unyielding sacrifice—not only from him, but from his wife and child—had closed her mouth just as tightly. Two husbands, two different silences. She wondered if it was simply her destiny to keep the secrets of men.

She felt loyalty to Mathias. She did. She admired his devotion, his goodness, the way he believed in something larger than himself. But she also hid from him. She hid her disobedience, her fear, her hunger. She wondered how long it would take before word reached him—that his wife had been seen at the market, that she had purchased food she should have easily had access to on their farm, that the baker's wife had called her out publicly to shame the Stirnimann family name. The constant fear of being exposed gnawed at her, day and night.

So she decided not to go anymore. Better to avoid the farmers' market altogether than to risk another whisper that might travel back to him. Instead, she began to watch the farm itself—the storehouses, the sheds, the henhouses, the places where food passed from hand to hand. She did not *want* to steal—she had never stolen anything in her entire life up until now. In fact, the thought had not even crossed her mind until Uli *der Leutknecht* gave it to her.

One morning he left a basket of small red potatoes by the wash house. He set it down as though by accident, but when he straightened, he caught her eye. There was something in his look—a quiet offering, a kind of permission. Then he hurried off before anyone could see.

Elisabetha waited. When the yard was empty, she walked over swiftly, lifted the basket and carried it through the back door of the kitchen, her heart pounding. She took it straight to the cellar and hid it with the little that remained from her trip to the farmers' market. She stood there a long moment, her hands trembling. She had crossed a line, though she could not yet name it.

After that, she began to notice things she had not seen before. The *Knechte* often left the storehouse doors slightly ajar. A sack of oats unguarded. A crate of pears cooling in the shade. Walnuts spread on a cloth to dry out. She learned to move quietly, to watch the corners of the yard, to slip inside only when she would not be seen. Her apron had deep pockets; she filled them with whatever she could carry—potatoes, turnips, pears, apples, walnuts, flour, oats. Sometimes she ducked into a henhouse and gathered a few eggs, as fast as a fox slipping past the henhouse door.

Cheese and meat were harder to purloin. Those huts were busy, the workers always coming and going. But now and then Elisabetha found a small wedge of cheese left on a table, or a couple of sausages, or a strip of fatty bacon. She took only what she could conceal. After a while she began to wonder if the *Knechte* were helping her—leaving things where she might find them, turning their backs at just the right moment. No one said a word. No one ever would.

She knew she was stealing. She knew it was a sin. But she told herself it was only right that she and her son should have a little nourishment. They were the wife and child of the master, after all. And Mathias gave so freely and generously to the poor that surely a few potatoes, a handful of oats, a wedge of cheese would not be missed.

Still, every time Elisabetha went to confession at the Marienkirche in Bertiswil, she felt the weight of it. She knelt on the worn *prie-dieu* before her confessor, Pater Alois Birrer, who sat in a simple wooden chair turned sideways, his ear angled toward her so she would not have to meet his eyes. Her hands were cold, her voice barely above a whisper.

"*I have stolen food.*"

She did not say from whom. She did not need to. Priests in tiny hamlets such as Bertiswil almost always knew. They knew their parishioners, their troubles, the stories behind them. Pater Birrer most certainly did.

Elisabetha wondered what he would say. Restitution was the usual penance for theft. But how could she make restitution to her own husband without revealing everything? Would her confessor truly demand it? Everyone knew Mathias's zeal, his endless charity, the way he fed every person in need from miles around while his own family lived on carrots and a handful of grain.

"*I am angry with God. I cannot pray anymore. My lips say the prayers, but my heart is empty. I blame Him for letting us starve.*"

Admitting these things in confession was much harder than admitting she was a thief. Everyone knew how grave such doubts were.

When she had finished whispering her litany of transgressions, Pater Birrer was silent for a long moment. He kept his eyes lowered. Then he murmured softly, "The Lord sees you, my daughter. You are forgiven your sins. Let us both pray every day for His mercy, and that God will heal Mathias."

Her breath caught. She had not spoken her husband's name. Had not breathed a word of him. Yet Pater Birrer knew. And in that knowing she felt the weight of it all—the isolation, the hunger, the fear. There was no hiding. Not from God. Not from any man of God. He rapidly gave her absolution, and she rose from her knees and bolted from the church.

That night Elisabetha lay awake beside her husband, listening to the slow rise and fall of his breath. She wondered if he would ever learn what she had done, slipping food into her apron, hiding it in the cellar, feeding the boy and herself in secret. She had never dreamed that his charity, his goodness, his endless sacrifices would become a burden she alone must bear.

Chapter Twenty-Two
Der Weg

The morning broke pale over Bertiswil, a thin wash of light across the fields. Mathias Stirnimann stood in the yard with his *Amtsbuch* under his arm and looked at the road that ran east toward Sins. He had taken the post of justice of the peace—*Friedensrichter*—several months before his marriage to Elisabetha, though he had not needed extra work.

Running the farm alone was enough to fill a man's days. But Mathias had wanted to greatly increase the number of good works he did after his meeting with the saintly Marguerite Bays. He had wanted to pour himself out completely until God Himself took notice.

Being a justice of the peace was not easy, to say the least. And it only carried a token stipend. He knew that. Yet he had accepted the burden without hesitation, as though the weight of it might balance the losses he carried.

His boots were already worn at the heels. He had gone through three pairs since spring. His *Knechte* said the roads knew his boots better than they knew the wheels of any cart. Mathias nodded. A *Friedensrichter* must go where he is needed.

He set out most days before the sun had cleared the ridge. The frost on the grass crackled under his steps. He walked with a steady, deliberate pace, like a man taught by sorrow to take no step lightly. The *Amtsbuch* thumped lightly against his ribs. Inside were the names of men who quarreled over land and water and inheritance, men who could not settle their own disputes and therefore called for him.

He passed the churchyard where Emerenzia and their three *Töchterli* lay. He did not look toward their graves. He never did. But he felt them, as he always felt them, like cold fingers pressed against his heart. He had made a vow there once. A bargain with God. *Take no more from me, and I will give all that I have. I will feed the poor. I will clothe the needy. I will empty my barns if I must. Only spare the ones who remain.*

He believed God had heard him. He believed God had agreed.

So he trudged on.

The first dispute of the day was at the farm of the *Gebrüder* Huber. They stood in the yard with their arms folded, each glaring at the other as though the devil himself had taken up residence in the other's skull. The petty quarrel was over a strip of pasture land no wider than a wagon's axle. Mathias listened to them in silence, his enormous hands clasped behind his back. When they had finished, he walked the length of the disputed ground, his boots sinking into the damp earth. He measured the distance with his stride, then returned to the brothers.

"You will divide it," he said. "Half to each. And you will shake hands before I leave."

They obeyed. They always did. There was something in the voice of *der Riese von Bertiswil* that made men listen.

He wrote their names and his verdict in the *Amtsbuch* and moved on.

By midmorning he was on the road again, the sun climbing, the frost melting into mud. He wiped his boots on the grass and kept walking. A *Friedensrichter* must not complain. He must not show weariness. He must be the still point in the turning world.

At the Müller farm he settled a quarrel over a debt. At the Schneider place he mediated a dispute about a broken fence and a cow that had wandered into the wrong field. At each stop he listened, he judged, he wrote. His voice was calm, his words measured. He carried the law in his head and the weight of the community on his shoulders.

But beneath it all, another weight pressed harder on him since his marriage to Elisabetha.

He thought of the thinness in her face. Of the way she humbly bowed her head when she served their meager meals. He thought of Kandid's hollow cheeks and quiet hunger. He told himself they were necessary sacrifices, a test of faith. God would see their suffering and reward it. God would protect them as long as Mathias kept his vow.

If I give enough, God will not take them from me.

He repeated it like a prayer.

At midday he sat on a stone wall and ate the burnt and discarded heel of a loaf of bread and a few slices of dried apple he removed from his pocket. He chewed slowly, watching the wind move through the bare branches. He thought about his first wife Emerenzia again. Of the fever that had taken her. Of the three small graves beside hers. He had not been able to save them. He had not given enough then. He had not known.

He closed his eyes. *Not again*, he thought. *Never again.*

A cart rattled past on the road. The driver lifted a hand in greeting. Mathias nodded and rose to his feet. There were still two more farms to visit before dusk.

At the Widmer place he found a husband and wife shouting across the yard. The wife accused the husband of giving too much to the church, of leaving their children hungry. The husband said God demanded sacrifice. Mathias felt a coldness settle in his chest. He heard the echoes of his own words. He listened to them argue, their voices sharp as knives. He saw the thinness of the children standing behind their mother.

He lowered his eyes and spoke quietly. "A man must care for his own household first. Charity begins at home."

The words hung in the air. He felt them strike him like a stone. He knew he did not practice what he preached. He knew his family's hunger was not temporary, not some passing season of want. In his own house, he kept his vow to God with a rigidity that left no room for softness, no room for mercy. And the knowledge of it—the hypocrisy of his own words—settled upon him.

He wrote the Widmers' names in the *Amtsbuch* with a hand that trembled once, then steadied. He closed the book and left without looking back.

The road home was long. The sun dipped behind the ridge, and the air grew cold again. His boots were heavy with mud. His legs ached. He walked with his head bowed, the book pressed against his side like a second heart.

He thought once more of the Widmer children. He thought of Kandid. He thought of the words he had spoken—words he himself did not follow. *A man must care for his own household first. Charity begins at home.* He wondered if God had heard him. He wondered if God had judged him.

But then an image of the graves flashed before his eyes. And the fear rose in him like a tide. He quickened his pace.

When he reached Ottorüthi, the lamps were lit in the windows. The yard was quiet. He entered the house and hung his coat on the peg. Elisabetha looked up from the table. Her face was pale in the lamplight. Kandid sat beside her—too quietly for a child his age—his hands folded in front of him.

Mathias murmured a greeting to them both. Then he went to wash his hands and face from the grime of the road.

Later, when the house was dark, he knelt beside the bed and repeated his usual prayers. His voice was a whisper, barely audible. Elisabetha lay still, pretending to sleep.

He prayed for strength.

He prayed for forgiveness.

But most of all, he prayed that God would not take his family from him again.

Outside, the wind moved like a slow blade through the trees. Inside, the house was silent except for the sound of Mathias Stirnimann's muted, desperate prayers.

Chapter Twenty-Three
Die Heimkehr

The night settled early over Ottorüthi, the inky darkness pressing against the windows. Mathias sat at the table long after the lamps had been snuffed, his *Amtsbuch* open before him. He had not written a word. The ink in the well waited silently. His hands rested on either side of the book as though he were holding something steady that wished to move.

The house was quiet. Elisabetha had taken herself to bed hours earlier. He could hear the faint creak of the rafters, the soft settling of the stones in the hearth. It was the kind of silence that made a man aware of his own breathing.

He closed the book and pushed it aside. The words he had spoken to *Bauer* Widmer a few days before still clung to him like burrs—they continued to haunt him. *Charity begins at home.* He had said it without thinking, the way a man repeats a proverb learned in childhood. But the moment the words left his mouth, he had felt something inside him break, as though a beam in the rafters had cracked under its own weight.

He now rose from the table and crossed the room. The floorboards were cold beneath his feet. He stood at the window and looked out into the yard. The moon was thin, a sliver of bone above the ridge. The wind moved like a cold hand through the trees.

He thought of the Widmer children, their hollow faces turned toward him. He thought of the husband's stubborn pride, the wife's trembling anger. He had seen himself, his wife, and his child in them—the man who believed sacrifice was holy, and the woman and child who bore the cost of it. The thought now turned his stomach.

He pressed his forehead against the glass; it was smooth and cold against his skin. His breath fogged the pane.

Once more, his mind returned to the vow he had made. A vow spoken in the shadow of three small graves. A bargain with God born of fear, not faith. He had promised God everything he had, everything he could give, if only He would spare the ones who remained. Surely his vow would keep death at bay.

But such vows had a way of turning on a man.

He stepped away from the window and walked to the hearth. The embers glowed faintly, a dull red pulse.

He crouched and stirred them with the poker, watching the sparks rise and die. He felt the heat on his face, but it did not reach the cold inside him.

He remembered Emerenzia's last days—the fever, the stillness, the way her breath had grown thin as thread. The memory of his three baby daughters never ceased to haunt him—each smaller than the last, their bodies light as bundles of linen in his arms when he carried them to the churchyard. He had not been able to save them. He had not known how to bargain with God then.

He knew now. And he could not—would not—forget.

He rose and went to the bedroom. The door creaked softly as he pushed it open. Elisabetha lay on her side, her back to him, her long thick braid splayed out upon the pillow. The room felt colder without the small sounds of a child sleeping nearby. Kandid had been moved to the little room off the hall, where boys his age belonged. Mathias could not hear his breathing. That small distance unsettled him, though he was loath to admit it.

He stood in the doorway a long time. He could see the outline of Elisabetha's shoulder beneath the blanket, the narrowness of her frame. She had grown thinner since summer. He had noticed it in small ways—the way her dress hung, the way her hands trembled when she lifted the kettle. He had told himself it was the season, the work, the demands of the household. He had told himself God would provide.

He stepped inside and knelt beside the bed. His knobbly knees ached on the wooden floor. He clasped his hands and bowed his head.

He did not pray aloud. The words would not come. They gathered in his throat, heavy and shapeless. The silence held him—at this moment, he feared it more than the graves.

After a long while he rose again and stepped into the hall. The door to Kandid's room was slightly ajar. A faint sliver of light from the kitchen stove reached the threshold. Mathias paused there, listening. The boy's breathing was soft, steady, distant. He did not enter. He only stood in the doorway, his hand on the frame, feeling the familiar ache of fear.

Then he turned away and went back to the darkened room where his wife slept. He sat on the edge of the bed, elbows on his knees, hands clasped. He knew what he had done. He knew what he continued to do. He knew the cost of his vow, and yet he knew he would not break it. Not even for them.

Especially not for them. The vow was the only thing he believed could keep them alive.

Mathias closed his eyes. The house was silent. The wind moved outside, restless in the trees. A hound dog bayed in the distance. Still, the night pressed close around him.

He sat there a long time, listening to the breathing of his wife and his son, the two lives he had sworn to protect with a sacrifice they did not understand.

He did not pray again. He did not sleep.

He only sat, holding the weight of his vow like a stone in his hands, knowing it would not lighten, knowing he would carry it as long as he drew breath.

Chapter Twenty-Four
The Barn Library

The first winter after Elisabetha's and Mathias's wedding came early, a hard white season that pressed itself against the windows and settled deep into the folds of the land. Snow lay over Ottorüthi like draped linen, and the days passed in a pale hush. It was in that quiet that Mathias told his wife what he had arranged.

He stood in the doorway of the kitchen, stamping the cold from his boots, and told her he had instructed Uli, his trusted *Leutknecht*, along with two of the younger *Knechte*, to clear the small west barn. He had told the men to seal it against the drafts, to make it tight and warm so that his wife's books would not be damaged by the cold or rain. They had even set traps and sealed it against mice. Then they were to build shelves—proper shelves, sturdy and tall—for the books.

"Winter on the farm is the time for such projects," Mathias said with a shy grin. "There will be room enough for all of them, and more besides. You should go and see that my men build them correctly, *min Schatz*. You will know best how such things ought to be done."

Elisabetha had not expected this. She had thought her books would remain in crates for years, tucked beneath the eaves or stacked in corners where rodents might find them. But her husband spoke as though the matter were simple, as though a library on a farm were as ordinary a thing as a new fence or a repaired roof.

The next morning she took Kandid by the hand and walked to the west barn. The air was sharp, the snow creaking beneath their boots. Inside, the men had already been at work for some time. She found the *Knechte* sweeping the floor clean after their repairs. They had stacked her crates in neat rows along the walls. There were more of them than she remembered—heavy wooden boxes bound with iron, each one nailed shut with a finality that suggested they had been meant to stay closed for a long period of time.

Opening them was no small task. Uli fetched a crowbar, and the first crate groaned as he pried it open, the nails resisting before they finally gave way. The lid came off with a crack, and the smell of old paper rose into the cold air—dry, sweet, unmistakable. Elisabetha felt something tighten in her throat. These were the books she had painstakingly wrapped in linen and brought from Sins, the books her first husband had collected with such care, the books she had once read in a quiet townhouse where she had been a different woman.

Kandid peered into the crate, his mittened hands gripping the edge.

"Mama…*so vil*," he whispered.

"*Ja,* so many," she echoed.

The *Knechte* lifted the books out one by one, handling them with a reverence that surprised her. They did not know the titles, but they understood the weight of them, the strangeness of so many bound volumes in a farmer's barn. They unwrapped each book slowly from its linen cloth. Leather bindings creaked in the cold.

Only after the crates were opened and the books stacked did the men return to the shelves. They measured the walls again, adjusting their earlier plans now that they could see the true size of the collection. The hammering resumed, slow and steady, echoing through the rafters. Boards were lifted, fitted, nailed into place. The barn changed shape under their hands.

Elisabetha stood with Kandid beside her, watching the shelves rise.

It felt like watching a house being built—one meant not for animals or tools, but for books.

When the last shelf was secured, Uli wiped his brow with the back of his sleeve and asked how she wanted the books arranged. He held a volume out to her, the spine turned upward, the letters meaningless to him.

She realized then that this task was hers alone.

She knelt on the cold floor and began sorting the books into rough categories—*Dichtung*, *Geschichte*, *Naturkunde*, *Geographie*—her fingers growing numb as she worked. The piles grew around her like small towers. Kandid sat beside her, stacking a few small volumes into towers of his own that immediately toppled.

It took many hours just to sort them.

It would take days to alphabetize them.

Uli, seeing how high the upper shelves reached, built his mistress a rolling ladder from leftover timber. It ran smoothly along the rail he fixed beneath the rafters. When Elisabetha climbed it for the first time, she felt a strange lightness, as though she were rising into a world made entirely of paper and ink.

When the shelves were finally ready, she began the slow work of placing each book in its proper place. The barn grew warmer with the labor, the air filled with the scent of pine boards and old leather.

Later that week, when the shelves were nearly full, Mathias had her first husband's *Biedermeier* desk carried into the barn. She watched as the men maneuvered it through the wide doors, its polished cherry wood catching the winter light. She had not seen it in over a year—not since it had been loaded onto the moving wagon in Sins. The sight of it here, in this cold barn in Bertiswil, stirred something she could not name—neither sorrow nor longing, but a faint ache of recognition.

The upholstered chairs from Josef's library followed, their fabric faded but still soft.

She placed them around the desk, arranging the small space as though it were a comfortable room inside a house, not a barn.

When she stepped back, she saw it clearly: a library, not improvised but made—built plank by plank, book by book, memory by memory.

Whenever her chores allowed, Elisabetha brought Kandid with her to the library. She settled him on a blanket with a wooden horse or a handful of toy blocks, and he played quietly while she read.

Sometimes she lifted him onto her lap and read aloud, her voice soft in the stillness, the words rising like breath in the cold air. The boy leaned against her, warm and trusting, his small fingers tracing the edges of the pages.

Word of the library spread quickly. First the *Knechte* came, caps in hand, to admire what they had built. Then neighbors from Bertiswil drifted in, curious and shy. No one had ever seen so many books gathered in one place. They stood before the shelves as though before an altar, whispering to one another, afraid to touch anything.

From that winter on, people began to refer to Elisabetha as *die Bibliothekarin von Bertiswil*—the librarian of Bertiswil. To her face she was still *Frau* Stirnimann, but the name clung to her gently, like snow on a sleeve.

Elisabetha told every visitor they were welcome to borrow books whenever they wished. She kept a small ledger on the *Biedermeier* desk, ready to record titles and names. But the pages remained empty. No one asked to borrow even a single book. It dawned on her that most could not read the titles, let alone the words inside. Many Swiss countryfolk could not even write their own names.

It was then that an idea took hold of her, quiet but persistent.

What if she were to ask Mathias for money to buy primers, catechisms, children's readers—books that could teach the illiterate to read and write? Books that might open the world a little wider for those who had never held a book in their hands?

But she hesitated. If Mathias would not adequately feed his own household, would he not think this a foolish expense? Would he see it as vanity, or worse, frivolity?

She began to consider how best to ask him.

Not at night, when he was tired and careworn, sunk deep in his own thoughts.

Not in the morning, when the day's burdens pressed close.

Perhaps on a Sunday, when the world felt softer, and the sound of the church bells lingered in the air like a promise.

Until then, she would wait.

Chapter Twenty-Five
The Asking

Sunday came gray and still, the kind of winter afternoon when the world seemed to hold its breath. Snow lay in soft drifts along the eaves, and the bells from Bertiswil carried faintly across the fields, their sound stretched thin by distance and cold. Inside the house, the fire burned low, giving off more light than warmth.

Elisabetha waited until the dishes were washed and set to dry, until Kandid had wandered off to play with his wooden farm animals near the stove, until Mathias had settled at the table with a small knife and a stick of wood he meant to carve. His shoulders were relaxed, his face unguarded. It was the moment she had been waiting for.

She dried her hands on her apron and stood for a long moment, steadying herself.

"Mathias," she said softly.

He looked up at once. "*Ja, min Schatz?*"

She sat across from him, folding her hands in her lap. "I have been thinking," she began, "about the library. About the people who come to look at the books."

He nodded, the knife paused in his hand.

"They admire them," she said. "But they cannot read them. Most cannot even write their own names."

Mathias's brow furrowed, not in displeasure, but in thought. He was an educated man, and he understood what it meant to live without letters.

"I would like to teach them to read and write," she said. "If you would allow it. If you would help me buy the books and materials I need—primers, catechisms, small readers for beginners, slates, chalk, paper, pencils."

The room grew very quiet. Even Kandid seemed to sense the stillness, his wooden goat held motionless in his hand.

Mathias set the knife down and leaned back in his chair. He regarded his wife with a seriousness that made her heart beat faster.

"Do you really want to take on such a task?" he asked. "Teaching grown men and women their letters is no small thing. They will be shy of it. And it will take time."

"I know," she said. "But I believe I can do it. And our son is beginning to notice the letters," she added softly. "He sits with me when I read. He could learn a little, alongside the others."

Mathias studied his wife's face, weighing her words with the steady intelligence she had admired in him from the beginning. Something softened in his expression—a small, unmistakable pride.

"If this is what you want," he said slowly, "then I will buy what you need. It is a good thing, to teach others. A charitable thing." He hesitated, then added, "And it would please me—and the Lord—to see you do it."

The words settled between them like warm air rising from the stove.

"You will need benches," he said after a moment, thinking it through. "People cannot stand through their lessons. I will have Uli build them before the cold grows worse."

Elisabetha felt a quiet loosening inside her, a release she had not expected. "Thank you," she said. "Truly."

Mathias nodded once, firmly, as though sealing the decision. "We will go to Rothenburg next week. The booksellers there will have what you need."

She bowed her head in gratitude, though she did not trust herself to speak again. Across the room, Kandid resumed his play, his small wooden farmyard animals clattering softly against the floorboards.

Later, when the house had grown dim and the fire had burned low, Elisabetha stepped out into the cold. The sky was a deep, unbroken gray, and the barn stood dark against the snow. She imagined the shelves inside, the rolling ladder, the quiet rows of books waiting to be read.

Soon, she thought.

Soon the barn would be warm with voices.

Soon the letters would come alive beneath unsteady hands.

Soon the world would widen for others, even if only by a little.

She pulled her shawl tighter around her shoulders and went back inside the house, carrying the promise of that future with her.

Chapter Twenty-Six
Christmas at the Villiger Farm

The snow fell in a fine, steady veil that Christmas morning as the Stirnimann family set out for Geltwil. The night before, they had kept their own *Heiligaabig* in Bertiswil, attending Midnight Mass at the Marienkirche and returning home through the cold, candlelit dark. Now, in the pale winter morning, Mathias hitched the mare to the small sleigh, brushing the frost from the leather traces with the flat of his hand. The air was sharp enough to sting the lungs, but the sky was clear, a washed winter blue that made the fields shine like hammered tin.

Elisabetha bundled Kandid into his thickest coat and scarf, pulled his *Wollmütze* low over his ears, and tucked his mittened hands beneath the thick *Pelzdecke* in the sleigh. His cheeks were already pink with cold, his breath rising in small clouds. He clutched the wooden horse his papa had carved for him, its edges worn smooth by his hands.

They set off just after sunrise, the runners whispering over the snow. The road wound past bare orchards and shuttered farmhouses, past the frozen Reuss where the ice lay in long, cracked sheets. Elisabetha watched the familiar landmarks pass—the bend in the road where she had gathered wildflowers as a girl, the low stone wall where she had sat to rest on summer walks. Each one felt both near and impossibly distant.

Geltwil appeared at last, its few clustered houses huddled against the cold. Beyond it, the land opened again into rolling fields and scattered farms. The Villiger place stood alone at the edge of a small wood, its roof heavy with snow, smoke rising thinly from the chimney. Even from a distance, the house looked orderly, prosperous, well-kept—the kind of farm that had weathered generations without slipping.

As they approached, Elisabetha felt a tightening in her chest. She had not realized how much she had changed until she saw the house again—the same low eaves, the same wooden shutters, the same worn threshold smoothed by generations of feet. It looked smaller than she remembered, or perhaps she had simply grown.

Her mother opened the door before they reached it. “Lisbeth,” she said, her voice catching. She drew her daughter into her arms, holding her longer than usual, as though measuring the thinness of her beneath the layers of wool.

Her father greeted Mathias with a firm handshake, his eyes flicking briefly—too briefly—over Elisabetha and Kandid. He said nothing, but the silence was heavy with what he did not ask. Mathias handed him their gifts—a bundle of firewood and a carved wooden ladle—without ceremony. Her father accepted both with a single nod, the kind that carried more weight than words.

Inside, the warmth was almost overwhelming. The kitchen smelled of cloves, cardamom, and roasted apples, of *Christstollen* pulled fresh from the oven. A small fir tree stood in the corner, its branches hung with white candles, dried orange slices, foil-wrapped chocolates, and bits of tinsel. Beneath it lay a few modest gifts.

Appollonia Villiger reached beneath the tree and brought out three small parcels. For Kandid, a matching knitted cap and mittens, the wool thick and soft, and a paper twist filled with tiny chocolate stars that made his eyes widen. For Elisabetha, a neat stack of lavender soaps, tied together with twine—Appollonia's own work, the scent familiar and almost unbearably tender. For Mathias, a black woolen scarf, tied with ribbon. He accepted it with a quiet "*Danke*," his face unreadable.

Kandid stared at the table laid out with food—real food, abundant and fragrant. Before Elisabetha could stop him, he reached for a slice of the glazed *Stollen*. He ate too quickly, swallowing in greedy mouthfuls.

"*Langsam, Büebli,*" she whispered, touching his shoulder. But it was too late. His small face went pale, and he pressed a hand to his stomach. Elisabetha's mother guided the child gently to a chair, murmuring soft reassurances in the old *Aargauer* dialect. The room fell quiet.

Johann Villiger's gaze met his daughter's across the table—a brief, sharp flash of understanding, of worry, of something like sorrow. He looked away at once.

The festivities resumed, but the earlier cheer had thinned. Conversation drifted to safer topics—the weather, the harvest, the new *Pfarrer* in Muri—yet beneath it all ran a current of unspoken questions.

Later, after the dishes were cleared and the candles lit, her mother drew Elisabetha aside. She did not speak. Her eyes moved over her daughter's face, her hands, the thinness of her shoulders beneath the wool. Then she nodded once, as though she had gathered all she needed to know.

"Mathias is a good man," Elisabetha murmured in response to Mama's silent appraisal. That was true. But his goodness did not put food on the table. She could not possibly explain that to her mother.

Appollonia nodded, though her eyes lingered on Elisabetha's face with a searching tenderness.

When it was time to leave, her father walked them to the sleigh. He lifted Kandid in with gentleness, tucking the fur lap robe around the small boy. Then he placed a heavy parcel wrapped in brown paper in his daughter's arms. She could imagine what her mother had tucked inside: thick slices of the *Christstollen*, wrapped in waxy paper, a slab of fresh butter, a few dozen *Weihnachtsguetzli.*

"For the road," he said simply.

She understood. It was not for the road.

As they rode back toward Bertiswil, the sky darkening to a deep winter blue, Elisabetha held the parcel in her lap and felt the weight of it—heavier than the food it contained, heavier than anything her parents had said or left unsaid.

Beside her, Mathias kept his eyes on the road, the reins held steady in his hands. The mare's breath rose in white plumes before them, carrying them home through the gathering dusk.

Elisabetha looked back once, watching the faint glow of the Villiger farmhouse flicker and fade behind the trees. The warmth of her parents' hearth receded into memory, leaving only the cold air on her face and the quiet ache in her chest.

Ahead lay Ottorüthi, her future, the lessons yet to come.

Behind lay the life she had once known.

Between them, the snow fell softly, erasing the tracks of their passing.

Chapter Twenty-Seven
Lessons

The first to come were the *Knechte.*

It happened on a gray afternoon in early January, when the snow lay in soft drifts against the barn walls and the air smelled of cold wood and distant smoke. Elisabetha had gone to the library to straighten the shelves and sweep the floor, Kandid trailing behind her with his wooden cow toy in one hand and a crust of bread in the other. She had just lit the small oil lamp on the desk when she heard footsteps outside—hesitant, stopping and starting, as if the walkers were unsure whether to continue.

When she opened the door, three of the *Knechte* stood there, caps in hand, shifting their weight like boys caught where they did not belong. Uli was among them, his face red from the cold and from something like embarrassment.

"*Frau* Stirnimann," he said, eyes fixed on the floorboards. "The master told us…you might teach us our letters."

Elisabetha looked at them—grown men, broad-shouldered from years of labor, hands cracked from the winter cold—and saw the same flicker of emotion in each of their faces: hope, quickly smothered by shame.

"*Ja*," she said simply. Then she smiled. "Please come in."

They stepped inside as though entering a church, their boots leaving small puddles of melted snow on the wooden floorboards. Kandid climbed onto the chair beside the desk, swinging his legs and watching them with solemn curiosity.

Elisabetha opened the ledger—the one she had intended for borrowed books—and dipped her pen in a pot of ink. The page was clean, the lines straight. At the top, as she always did, she wrote the place:

Ottorüthi.

The old spelling needed no thought; it was simply the way the name had always been written in the parish books and land records, much older than the farm itself.

"Your names?" she asked.

One by one, they spoke them. She wrote each carefully, leaving space beside them for notes she did not yet know how to make. When she finished, she closed the ledger with a soft thud. The men watched her hands as though she were performing a kind of magic.

She began with the alphabet.

Elisabetha drew each letter slowly on a slate, her handwriting neat and deliberate.

"This one," she said, tapping the A, "is like the roof of a house. Sloped at the sides, meeting at the top."

Uli nodded, seeing it.

She pointed to the M. "Like the mountain peaks."

The E. "The tines of a rake."

The O. "A cheese wheel."

The men smiled—small, embarrassed smiles—but the shapes began to make sense.

"Now the sounds," she said.

She tapped the A again. "*Ah.*"

The men repeated it, their voices uneven—one too loud, one barely audible, one stumbling over the simple shape of the sound. She tapped the M. "*Mmm.* Like when you taste something good." They tried again, some with a kind of shy determination, others with the stiff caution of men unused to being taught something new.

Kandid joined in confidently, pleased to be doing what the grown men were doing. His small voice threaded through theirs, steady and sure.

Elisabetha blended the sounds. "*Mmm*...*ah*...Ma."

They followed her, haltingly at first, then with more certainty.

"*Sss*...*ah*...Sa."

"*Lll*...*ah*...La."

Slowly, the barn filled with the rough, earnest music of syllables finding their voices.

When they were ready, she showed them the printed forms of the letters from a prayer book and from the *Hinkender Bote*, the popular Swiss almanac that every household in the canton seemed to own. The men frowned at the ornate *Fraktur* shapes, but she guided them patiently, showing how each one grew from the simple Latin letters they were learning.

Then she handed each man a stick of chalk and a slate of his own—a simple wooden frame with a dark stone center, the kind every schoolchild used. The men held them awkwardly, like tools they had never seen before. It was their turn now—they would make their first marks.

The barn was quiet except for the scratch of chalk. Outside, the wind pressed against the walls, but inside, the air was warm with breath and concentration.

When the lesson ended, the men stood awkwardly, unsure how to leave.

"How often should we come?" one of them asked.

"Every day," Elisabetha replied. "If you want to learn, you must come often."

Each nodded his thanks in his own stiff way and filed out into the cold. She watched them go, their figures small against the white fields.

It was a beginning.

The next day, two more *Knechte* came.

The day after that, a *Bauernfrau* from the far end of Bertiswil, her shawl dusted with snow, asked if she might learn to read the almanac her husband brought home each year.

A week later, another woman came—then two neighbors, then a boy of twelve who had never held a slate.

Elisabetha taught them all.

For the men, she chose practical things: broadsheets from the *Gemeinde*, seed catalogues, notices about livestock.

For the women, whatever they wished: a psalm, a recipe, a letter from a sister in a faraway town.

Some wanted only to learn to sign their names. Others wanted more.

The ledger filled slowly, line by line, with names written in her careful hand. She left space beside each one for notes—progress, attendance, the first word read independently. Sometimes she added nothing at all. The names themselves were enough.

Kandid sat beside her through it all, solemn and watchful, tracing chalk shapes on his own little slate while the adults bent over theirs. He grew up in that barn, among the smell of chalk and ink, the murmur of halting voices sounding out their first words.

Outside, Ottorüthi remained what it had always been—fields, frost, the long grind of work—but inside the barn, something small and steady took root. It was a change so quiet it could be missed if one did not look closely.

Most lessons were taught in winter. In spring and summer there was less time; work took up their days. Still, the barn remained a place of learning, and the first ledger filled so completely that Elisabetha had to buy another.

Life went on this way for nearly three years, the days moving in a slow, steady rhythm. Later, when Elisabetha looked back, she would remember this time—the shy men at the door, the women with their shawls pulled tight, the scratch of chalk, the soft glow of the oil lamp—as the first quiet turning of her life that belonged wholly to her, something new and hopeful.

Chapter Twenty-Eight
The Knowing

Three years after her marriage, Elisabetha Stirnimann was forty-two years old and had long since accepted that she would never bear a child. It was not a sorrow she spoke aloud. It was simply a fact, like the cold in winter or the thinness of the soup. She told herself she was too old, and too hungry besides. Perhaps it was even the consequence of her loss of faith in God. Her monthly courses had grown irregular since her wedding—sometimes late, sometimes early, sometimes little more than a stain, sometimes nothing at all. She barely paid attention to them anymore. There was no reason to.

Mathias never raised the subject. He had accepted the matter with the same quietness he brought to everything. He did not scold her or sigh or look at her with disappointment. If he felt any grief about it, he kept it folded away, as he did with all things that troubled him.

Then, one February morning, Elisabetha woke with a strange heaviness in her limbs, as though her bones had been packed with sand. She sat up too quickly and the room tilted. A wave of nausea rose in her throat. She pressed a hand to her mouth and breathed through it until the feeling passed. She blamed the cold, or the crude porridge, or the long hours in the barn.

But the dizziness returned the next day. And the next.

Soon she was sick morning, noon, and night. Sometimes she vomited until her ribs ached. She dreamed of food—strange, impossible combinations—and woke gagging, her mouth full of bitterness.

She tried to hide her wretchedness from Mathias, but he simply watched her from the corner of his eye, saying nothing.

Elisabetha's cravings came without warning and made no sense. One afternoon she found herself longing for an entire bowl of sweet whipped cream — something she had never eaten in such abundance in her life. The thought of it made her mouth water and her stomach twist with hunger. Other cravings were simply bizarre. She imagined cold sauerkraut mixed with stewed cherries and drenched in chocolate sauce, the colors swirling together in a way that made her both queasy and yet strangely eager to taste it. She laughed at herself, embarrassed by the absurdity, knowing she would never eat such things.

Then, one afternoon, as she knelt to scrub the kitchen floor, a thought struck her so sharply she sat back on her heels. Could she be with child?

The idea seemed preposterous. She was too old. Too thin. Too worn. But the thought would not leave her. It glowed in her mind like a small, stubborn flame.

In those days, no one went to a doctor to confirm a pregnancy. Women simply waited to see if a child would grow.

For a week she said nothing. She watched her body with a kind of wary disbelief. Her breasts felt tender. Her belly, though still small, felt different beneath her hand—not larger, but stiffer, as if it were occupied. She moved more slowly without meaning to. She found herself listening to her own breath.

One morning, after rising from bed and steadying herself against a wave of nausea and vertigo, she turned to Mathias. He stood by the window, fastening his cuffs, pretending not to watch her.

"I am not certain," she said quietly. "But I think I may be with child."

Mathias looked up. A grin broke across his broad, plain face—sudden, unguarded, boyish. He had suspected it, but he had waited for her to speak first. He crossed the room in two strides and took her hands in his. He did not speak. He only embraced her, pressing her forehead against his chest, holding still as if the moment might break.

After that, everything changed.

Uli began bringing food each morning—real food, not scraps. Pork cutlets. Several varieties of cheese. Small bags of dried apples and pears. Even strings of smoked sausages. She had never been offered such an abundance since coming to Ottorüthi as a bride. He offered it all with a shy smile, his eyes bright with the secret he had been told.

Elisabetha thanked him, but being who she was, she shared this bounty with Kandid and Mathias. She ate more than before, but never enough to fully satisfy her and the strange cravings that seized her—dill pickles, chocolate bonbons, fish eggs. She laughed at herself every time such odd foods came to mind.

She continued teaching in the barn, though she tired more easily. The *Knechte* noticed her pallor and worked more quietly, as though afraid to disturb her. The women brought her small gifts—a jar of beef broth, a pot of dried herbs. She accepted them timidly but with gratitude.

The village midwife came to the house every few weeks. She was a stern woman with sharp eyes and a voice that brooked no argument. She frowned when she learned Elisabetha's age. She frowned at her small belly. She frowned at the thinness of her wrists.

"You must eat more," she said.

"I am—I am trying," Elisabetha replied.

The midwife snorted. "Try harder."

Despite this concern, the months passed, and the child grew—though slowly. Elisabetha felt the first fluttering movements in late summer—later than most women, the midwife said, but not surprising for a woman of her age and condition who was carrying her first child. It felt like a soft tapping, like a bird testing its wings. She pressed her hand to her belly and closed her eyes, feeling a warmth spread through her chest that she had never known before.

When November came, the woman told them it was time to send Kandid away for a few days. The boy hesitated, clinging to his mother's skirt. Even at five, he sensed the danger. He remembered little of his birth mother, only shadows and the smell of her milk, but he feared losing this mother, too.

"You will come back," Elisabetha told him, smoothing his hair. "We will be together again, *Büebli*. And when you return, there will be a little brother or sister here for you to meet, if God wills it." She hoped her words brought him some comfort. She was not certain God had a hand in any of it, though she would never dare to admit the thought to anyone.

He nodded wordlessly, though his eyes were wet.

After Mathias brought Kandid to his *Tante's* house, Ottorüthi felt too quiet. Elisabetha sat by the fire in the *Stube*, her hands folded over her belly, listening to the wind rattle the shutters. She felt the first pains that night—sharp, insistent, low in her back. She breathed through them, steady and silent, as the midwife had taught her.

The labor would be long. The child would be small. But she did not yet know that.

She only knew that something was coming—something she had never dared to hope for—and that she must meet it with courage and a steady heart.

Chapter Twenty-Nine
The Arrival

The house felt hollow without Kandid's small footsteps. His absence left a stillness that pressed against the walls, as though the air itself were waiting. Elisabetha sat, her hands folded over her belly, breathing through the low, steady pains that had begun the night before. They were not yet strong, but they were insistent, gathering themselves like a storm far off in the hills.

Mathias moved quietly around her, unsure where to put himself. He brought more wood for the fire, then stood with his hands on the back of a chair, watching his wife with a helplessness he tried to hide. When the midwife arrived just after dawn, stamping the snow from her boots, she took one look at Elisabetha and nodded.

"It will be today," she said.

She set down her bag and began to prepare the room. Mathias stepped forward, but the midwife lifted a hand.

"*Herr* Stirnimann, you must wait outside now," she said gently. "I will call you when it is time."

He obeyed without protest. Men had no place in childbirth.

He stepped into the cold morning and crossed the yard to the nearest barn, the only place where he could be alone with his fear. The animals stirred as he entered, shifting in their stalls. He knelt beside the feed trough, the straw pricking his knees, and took out his rosary. He prayed the decades slowly, methodically, the familiar rhythm steadying his breath. Outside, an uneasy stillness held. Inside the house, he could hear nothing.

He prayed until his fingers were numb, until he lost track of the hours, until the beads felt worn smooth beneath his thumb. Only when the barn door creaked open and the midwife's lantern appeared did he rise.

"Come now," she said. "They are safe. You have a daughter."

Inside, the *Schlafzimmer* was warm and dim. Elisabetha lay exhausted in the bed, but alive, her hair damp against her temples. In her arms was a small bundle wrapped in cloth. When Mathias stepped closer, the midwife shifted aside so he could see.

The baby was very small. Smaller than any newborn the midwife had delivered that year. Her limbs were thin, her face square, her neck short. She looked more like a bird fallen too soon from its nest than a child ready for the world.

But she breathed. And she cried—a thin, reedy sound, but a sound all the same.

Mathias reached out a tentative hand, touching the top of her head with that profound gentleness he possessed.

"She will need to be kept warm," the midwife said. "Very warm."

Before she left that night, the woman pulled Mathias aside.

"Your wife lost a great deal of blood," she said. "If she is to recover her strength and produce good milk, she must eat well. Meat, especially. As much as you can spare."

Mathias nodded, his face pale. A bead of cold sweat broke out on his forehead. He had not realized how close the danger had come.

The next morning, without a word, he brought Elisabetha a plate with the choicest cuts from the smokehouse—pieces he had never once taken for himself or his family. Uli looked surprised when he saw them, but Mathias only said, "My wife needs good meat. The midwife insisted."

For the first time in years, Elisabetha ate until she was full.

They named the baby the next day. Elisabetha chose Martina, after the third century Roman martyr she had first read about when she was a girl. Mathias insisted the child carry her name as well.

"She would not be here without you," he said simply.

So their daughter became Martina Elisabetha Stirnimann.

As the new mother held her infant, a strange old fear suddenly flashed through her mind—Josef, the pictures, the vow. She felt shocked that she would think about that now. It passed quickly, however—leaving her with the warm weight of the child and the rawness of her own body.

For a time, the household lived in a kind of fragile abundance. Uli continued to bring food each morning—flour with which to bake bread, sausages, wedges of cheese, a bag of dried apples and plums. Mathias encouraged it, believing it his duty to provide for the nursing mother. Elisabetha ate more than she had in years. Her milk was strong. The infant grew, though slowly. She continued to share this abundance with Kandid, too. Mathias typically rejected anything more she gave him, telling her tersely to save it for herself. Elisabetha accepted the extra food gratefully while it lasted.

In early spring, her *Aargauer* parents arrived for a visit in their horse cart just after midday. The first green shoots showed along the ditch banks, nothing more than a hint of color. The couple must have left Geltwil in the cool of the morning, the road long but familiar to people who had spent their entire lives traveling between farms and markets. Her father handled the reins with the easy confidence of a man accustomed to horses, and her mother climbed down without assistance.

They carried a basket between them—eggs cushioned in straw, a round goat cheese, a loaf of rye, fresh butter, a thick slab of bacon, cherry preserves, and a length of cured sausage. Not extravagant gifts, but the kind of nourishment they knew their daughter needed.

Inside, they stood for a moment, letting their eyes adjust. Appollonia took the baby first, holding her infant granddaughter with a practiced steadiness that pleased her daughter. "She is small," she murmured, "but she has strength in her cry."

Johann Villiger touched his grandchild's cheek with a work-roughened finger, then stepped back to study Elisabetha. "You look well," he said, though his eyes lingered momentarily on the shadows beneath her eyes.

They stayed only a few hours. The horse needed rest before the return journey, and there were animals waiting at home. Before they left, her mother pulled her aside. "Eat as much as you can," she counseled. "You will need it."

After the cart rattled down the lane, Elisabetha stood in the doorway for a long time, holding her baby and feeling the weight of her parents' unspoken worry.

As the months went on, the extra food began to dwindle. Not all at once. Just less grain, a little less cheese, a little less meat. Mathias resumed his old habits without noticing—giving away what he believed others needed more, trusting God to provide for his own household. Elisabetha felt the shift before anyone spoke of it. The portions grew smaller. The hunger crept back like a familiar shadow.

By the time Martina was weaned, nearly a year after her birth, the scarcity had fully returned. Elisabetha resumed her stealthy tactics—slipping extra bites to Kandid, saving the choicest bits for the baby, pretending she had already eaten. And when the hunger grew sharp, she returned to the activities she had only ever confessed to her parish priest: searching the barns and sheds for whatever the workers had left behind—a burnt loaf of bread, a handful of grain, a heel of cheese discarded on a shelf. She took only what would not be missed and what could be easily concealed in her apron pockets or beneath her cloak. She told herself it was not stealing if it kept her children fed.

One evening, as his baby daughter slept in her cradle, Mathias stood over her, studying her face in the lamplight. She was nearly a year old, and her features had settled into their lasting shape. He felt a tenderness toward her, fierce and protective. But a thought crossed his mind, unbidden and practical: *If her looks do not improve, I will need to put a great deal by for her dowry. I know how shallow men are.*

He felt no shame in the thought. It was simply the truth of the world, and it was his duty to prepare for it. It was of the utmost importance for one's daughter to secure a good husband, after all.

At church, the whispers returned. Elisabetha heard them behind her—the same voices, the same pitying tones.

"Mathias Stirnimann is a godly man, but I would not want to be his child. Or his wife."

Elisabetha kept her eyes on her prayer book and pretended she could not hear.

At home, she watched her tiny daughter sleep, her small chest rising and falling beneath the blanket. She watched Kandid eat his meager portion with the careful restraint of a child who knows there will be no more. She watched Mathias kneel by the bed each night, praying for the poor, the sick, the hungry—all those he believed needed more than he and his family did.

Sometimes she could feel her anger threatening to burst forth. In her mind she spoke the words she would never dare say aloud: *Do you know what your charity costs your own family? Do you ever pray that we can withstand the hunger you so freely impose upon us?*

The old dread settled back into her bones.

The hunger had returned.

The judgment had returned.

The quiet suffering of the household had returned.

Elisabetha held her daughter close, feeling the fragile warmth of her body, and wondered how she would keep both children safe in the hard days to come.

Chapter Thirty
The Reckoning

The years slipped by like shadows across the barn wall, and in their wake the children grew—but shaped by want. Elisabetha never bore another child. The two she had grew in spite of scarcity, though Kandid stretched into a scarecrow of a boy and Martina continued to carry the stunted look she had been born with. Their mother saw it. The neighbors saw it. Even strangers remarked on it. Only Mathias seemed blind—or else he chose blindness, turning his eyes from what stood before him.

Martina became her mother's mirror. By three and a half she could read—not merely children's tales, but some of the very books her mother read. She had already been taken to Rothenburg at the age of four to be fitted with spectacles by the oculist. In the barn library the mother and daughter sat side by side, their gold wire-rimmed frames glinting in the lamplight, pages turning in quiet harmony. Visitors smiled and nudged each other at the sight—the miniature mirroring the original, both absorbed in the printed page as though the world outside did not exist.

The two Stirnimann children were bound by blood and by want. Kandid, thin and sharp-eyed, kept close to his sister, watching over her with a vigilance learned too early. She leaned into him without question, and together they bore the knowledge of hunger that had marked their lives.

But hunger teaches children more than letters ever could. They had both discovered ways to feed themselves as they grew. Even the young Martina had learned to search the deep pockets of her father's coat in her parents' wardrobe after he returned from the road, sometimes finding the rare treasure of a crust of bread, a stray walnut half, or perhaps a sliver of dried apple.

At some point, the siblings had learned to thieve, just as their mother had been forced to do. By the ages of eleven and six, their boldness grew. On Saturdays during market season, they worked the Bertiswil farmers' market in tandem. Martina's cuteness and sweetness were their weapons—while she asked questions or smiled at the farmwives, Kandid's hand moved quickly. When the boy created a diversion by pretending to fall and bang his shin, Martina would dart behind a table and grab whatever she could get her hands on before stowing it in her apron pockets.

Flies buzzed around the cheese stall; the cheesemonger's wife waved them off with her kerchief. The market was crowded, the air thick with the smell of fruit and cheese. The sun was hot on their backs as the two carried home cream buns, slices of cheese, sausage links, and apple slices, eating their spoils along the way and washing them down with spring water and fruit plucked from someone else's orchard.

One morning, their luck failed. At the butcher's stall, Martina distracted the wife with chatter while Kandid reached for a smoked sausage ring hanging from a hook. The butcher returned from his cart at that very moment and caught the boy red-handed. In an instant, he had Kandid by the ear and Martina by the arm. They could not run. "Well now. *Bauer* Stirnimann's children. Caught in the act. I should've known."

He then marched the young culprits back to Ottorüthi, his grip like iron, and delivered them to their mother.

"These two are thieves. Caught them stealing my sausage. How many others have they robbed, eh?

Something must be done, *Frau* Stirnimann. I demand justice," the butcher spat angrily.

Elisabetha's horror was complete. She had never sanctioned this, but she knew at once where they had learned it. Guilt rose in her throat, thick and bitter.

The butcher would not leave, nor would he unhand the children. He demanded repayment, demanded punishment, and even offered to beat them himself.

"You will not lay a hand on them," Elisabetha answered, her voice flinty, though her hands trembled.

He scoffed. "They will never learn otherwise," he said. "The Bible says if you spare the rod, you'll spoil the child." He paused a moment.

"I would turn them in to the police, if I could. But there are none here. Only your husband, the *Friedensrichter*. And that is a lost cause, since they are his children."

He muttered an oath under his breath, released the two, turned on his heel, and stormed off.

After he left, Elisabetha stood in the kitchen, her hands pressed against the table to steady herself. She knew something drastic must be done. She could no longer carry this burden alone. Pater Alois Birrer was the only one who knew all of her secrets, and she knew that Mathias would be more likely to listen to him than to her. She sent the children to bed after an early supper.

When her husband returned home, she told him simply: "We must go to Pater Birrer. We must go *right now*." Elisabetha's voice carried a weight he had never before heard. He had no idea what had happened, but he obeyed her without question.

Elisabetha knocked on the dark wooden door of the rectory. Inside, they found the lamps lit and Pater Birrer sitting at his desk, an aged crucifix casting its shadow across the wall. Elisabetha did not wait upon ceremony. She broke at once, her angry words spilling out after nine years of silence.

"Now look what you have done, Mathias! Are you happy now? For nine years I have endured this misery, stealing what I could to keep our children alive. Do you think I fed us on baskets of carrots alone? I searched barns and sheds for scraps. And now what has happened? Our children have learned to steal as well! This is the fruit of your righteousness!"

Mathias's eyes bulged from their sockets. He was wild-eyed and confused. "*What has happened?* Tell me what's happened!"

"I'll tell you what's happened! The butcher dragged Kandid and Martina home today after catching them stealing sausages at the market. He caught them in the act! And they both confess it has been going on for some time—they have stolen food every Saturday morning at the farmers' market—from the butcher, the baker, the cheesemaker, and the fruit sellers. Why? Not because they are wicked. But because they are *hungry*. As I am. *All the time*."

Mathias Stirnimann, *der Riese von Bertiswil*, collapsed into a chair and cradled his head in his hands upon hearing his wife's angry torrent of words. His voice was low, almost broken. "I made a vow. Years ago, before the graves in the churchyard, after I spoke with Marguerite Bays. I swore before God to do as much good as I could. That is why I have given as much as I could to the poor. To save your life. And the lives of our children. So that I would not be punished again."

And then he wept.

Pater Birrer's voice was calm, but it cut like a blade. "Mathias, do not blame Marguerite Bays for your actions. I am certain she never told you to starve your wife and children. My son, you must learn this: God does not make bargains with us. Nor does he punish us by taking lives. His will is unknowable—mysterious. He is pleased by acts of goodness, yes—but do you think He is pleased that your children must steal food when your farm overflows with abundance? Do you think that God is pleased by the wretched *misery* of your wife, who has borne the burden of hunger for her children and herself for nine long years, because you have nearly starved them? Know this: Your extreme sacrifice at their expense is a kind of sickness. And it must stop today," the priest thundered in a tone that would brook no argument.

Mathias continued to sob quietly. Then he whispered, "*But I am afraid. Afraid that if I stop, God will punish me again. He will take them all from me. I could not bear it. I would die rather than lose them.*"

Elisabetha's voice was sharp, unsparing. "Without proper nourishment, you may lose them anyway. Do you not see? Your son looks like a scarecrow, and your daughter was born stunted, most likely because I did not have enough food when she was conceived. If they were to get the grippe, or some other sickness like measles, they would be so weak, they would almost certainly be carried off by it."

Pater Birrer leaned forward. "You do not need to feed half of Switzerland alone. Others will give, too, if you give them a chance. You *must* care for your own household first."

Mathias Stirnimann covered his face with his hands. His shoulders shook uncontrollably.

Elisabetha watched him, her anger now mingled with pity.

"And besides, Mathias," the priest said, "there are other ways to be of service to your fellow man—and who knows but that God will reveal them to you in time."

Now Pater Birrer rose from his chair.

"Come," he said. "Both of you. Into the church."

They followed him out of the rectory, through the sacristy's dim stillness, and into the dark nave, until they stood before the tabernacle. The lamp burned steadily, its flame reflected in the brass.

"Mathias," the priest instructed, "kneel."

Mathias bent his great frame to the stone floor. Elisabetha stood beside him, her hands clenched tight.

Pater Birrer spoke slowly, each phrase measured.

"Repeat after me. Lord Jesus Christ, present in this Holy Sacrament, I vow to care for the wife and children You have entrusted to me. I vow to share with them an abundance of food from the abundance You have freely and so generously given me. I vow to give to the poor as I am able, but never again to withhold food from my own household. May Thy will be done, not mine."

Mathias's voice trembled as he echoed the priest's words. When he finished, silence filled the church.

Pater Birrer laid a hand on his shoulder.

"From this day, Mathias, your vow is changed. It is no longer a bargain with God, but true obedience to Him."

Elisabetha closed her eyes. She felt the weight shift, as though something long pressing upon her had been lifted. Perhaps God had listened to her desperate pleas, after all. A small warmth stirred in her, something she had not felt in a long while.

From that moment forward, the spell of hunger was broken at Ottorüthi.

Chapter Thirty-One
The Aftermath

Sunday came quiet and hot. The barn roof shimmered in the early light. No one worked. No one sold. No one bought. The market stalls in Bertiswil stood empty as they always did on Sundays, their canvas awnings tied down against the wind.

Mathias had not slept. He rose before dawn, ready to go, ready to make things right—but the world would not change for him. He stood at the window, hat in hand, staring toward the road that led to the hamlet. Elisabetha watched him from the table, her hands wrapped around a cup of thin coffee. She knew what he was thinking.

"It cannot be done today," she said softly.

"I know."

He set his hat down with a sigh. His hands trembled. The heat pressed against the house, thick and unmoving. Mathias stood in the hard light, hands clasped behind his back, waiting for his children to gather.

The two came into the kitchen, still sleepy. Martina climbed onto her chair; Kandid hovered beside her, watchful as always. They looked at their father fearfully.

"We are sorry, Papa," Kandid said meekly. "Aren't we, Martina?" His sister nodded glumly, her lashes wet with tears, her childish lips trembling.

Mathias knelt before them, his great frame folding awkwardly.

"I am not angry with you, *Chinder,*" he said. "I am ashamed."

Martina blinked. "Of us?"

"Of myself." He took their hands in his—one small, one smaller. "You stole because I failed you. I failed my entire family."

Kandid swallowed. "We didn't want you and Mama to know."

"I understand," Mathias said. "But now I must ask something of you both. Tell me everything you took. Every bun, every sausage, every apple. And from whom."

The children exchanged frightened glances. Mathias knew then that the amount must have been considerable. Then, haltingly, they told him. The cream buns and *Gipfeli* from *Frau* Bieri's stall. The cheese samples from the cheesemaker's stall. The sausage strings from the butcher. The apples from the miller's wagon. The dried pears from Widow Imboden. And it had been going on every Saturday for many months.

Mathias listened without interrupting. When they finished, he nodded once.

"Thank you for telling me the truth," he said. "That is all I ask of you today."

He rose slowly, as though carrying a weight that had been years in the making—which it was.

The bells of the Marienkirche rang across the fields, calling the faithful to Mass as they did every Sunday. The Stirnimanns walked the road together—Mathias tall and rigid, Elisabetha pale but steady, the children pressed close to their mother's skirts.

People noticed. Of course, they noticed.

Two women slowed their steps as the family passed.

"*Did you hear—?*"

"*The butcher caught them—*"

"*Stealing sausage, of all things—*"

"*And the little girl too, imagine—*"

They did not bother to lower their voices.

Near the church door a man muttered, "*Friedensrichter*, eh? Can't even keep his own house in order."

Another answered, "God help us if he's fit to judge anyone."

Kandid heard. His face burned red. Martina clutched her brother's sleeve. Mathias kept walking, jaw tight, eyes fixed on the church steps. Elisabetha's hands trembled, but she did not falter.

Inside, the murmurs continued—not whispers, but the low, buzzing talk of a village that thrives on scandal. The Stirnimanns took their usual place, third pew from the back, left side. The air around them felt charged, like a storm waiting to break.

Then Pater Birrer entered. He saw everything. He heard everything. He always did.

He stepped to the lectern, where the great lectionary lay open, its heavy pages edged in red. He paused long enough that the church fell quiet. The brass sanctuary lamp flickered beside the tabernacle, casting a steady glow.

He turned a few pages, and then his voice carried through the nave: "A man had two sons…"

The parable of the Prodigal Son. He read it slowly, deliberately, letting each line settle into the rafters.

When he closed the enormous book, he looked out over the pews at his parishioners. His gaze passed over the Stirnimanns without lingering, but the weight of it was unmistakable.

His homily was short.

"There are times when a man, even with the best of intentions, loses his way. Times when a family suffers for reasons unseen. Times when fear or misguided zeal leads to harm. But God does not turn His face from those who return to Him. And neither should we. We are quick to judge, quick to speak cruel words, slow to understand. But forgiveness is not optional for Christians. It is *commanded*."

Pater Birrer's final words thundered throughout the small church. He did not name Mathias. He did not name Elisabetha. He did not name the children. He didn't need to.

The loud talk stopped. The snickering died. The gossip shrank to a mutter.

But forgiveness? That would take years. These provincial villagers would soften, eventually. They would nod in greeting again. But the memory of the scandal would cling like smoke to their clothes.

The week that followed was long.

Too long.

The waiting became its own penance.

Mathias went about his work with a heaviness that startled even Uli. He ate little. He spoke less. At night he lay awake beside Elisabetha, staring at the ceiling beams, hearing the echo of his own words in the church: *I vow to care for the wife and children You have entrusted to me.*

He watched his children eat—finally eat until they were satisfied—and the joy on their faces was a knife in his heart, underscoring his guilt. He watched Elisabetha's quiet relief, and that was another knife. He watched Uli bring provisions with a broad grin, and he knew how easily he could have allowed this years ago.

He sat with it.

He could not escape it.

On the next Saturday, he rose before dawn.

The time was now.

He walked to Bertiswil somberly, each step heavier than the one before it. The market was already stirring—the butcher sharpening his knives, the cheesemaker's wife arranging cheeses, the miller unloading sacks of grain.

Mathias went first to the butcher.

The man looked up, cleaver in hand. "*You*," he snarled.

Mathias ignored his rudeness. He set the coins on the counter—more than the cost of many strings of stolen sausages. "I've come to repay what my children took."

"That's more than triple."

"*Ja*."

"And what of punishment? A hard whipping would do them both the world of good."

Mathias lifted his gaze. "If you wish to beat someone, beat me. I am the one at fault."

The butcher scoffed. "You'd let me strike you?"

"If it would satisfy you," Mathias said quietly. "But you will not lay a hand on my children. Do you understand?"

The butcher hesitated, thinking for a moment of the strength of the man standing in front of him, recalling that he was known as *der Riese von Bertiswil.* Then he grunted. "Get out of my sight," he said through his teeth, an ugly sneer twisting his features. And keep your children out of my stall."

Mathias humbly bowed his head. "Thank you."

He went next to the cheesemaker's stall, and then to the miller's wagon. At each place he repeated the same ritual: hat in hand, humble apology spoken plainly, coins offered without excuse.

Some vendors were gracious.

Some were cold.

One woman crossed herself and said, "God bless you for coming."

Another muttered sourly, "It's about time."

Mathias accepted it all, his head bowed in penance.

The Widow Imboden was last.

She sat at her small table, arranging her dried pears in neat piles. Her hands were gnarled and slow with age. When she saw Mathias approaching, she straightened.

He laid the coins on the table.

"*Frau* Imboden," he said quietly. "My children stole from you. I've come to make amends."

Her eyes widened. "*Ach*, *Herr* Stirnimann…*nai*. Keep your money. They were hungry. I would have *given* my fruit to them, had they asked."

Mathias shook his head. "You should not have had to."

She pushed the coins back toward him. "I have little, but I do not begrudge starving children. Truly, I don't."

He picked up the coins, took one of her hands, placed them into her palm, and closed her fingers around the money, gently but firmly.

"Please. Take it. I cannot leave here owing you."

She gave him a small, tired smile. "You are a good man, Mathias Stirnimann. You only lost your way."

His voice broke on the answer.

"No. I lost sight of what matters most."

The widow's expression softened. "Then God has brought you back to it."

Mathias bowed his head. Suddenly, he did not trust himself to speak. His shame was sharp and clean—that a woman with so little had shown more mercy than he ever had.

When he returned home, the sun was low. Elisabetha met him at the gate.

"Well?" she asked.

"It is done," he said.

She studied his face—the exhaustion, the humility, the strange peace beneath it. She nodded once, and that was enough. Then she took his hand.

The next morning, Uli arrived with a basket filled to bursting. Eggs. Cheese wrapped in cloth. A slab of cured ham. New red potatoes. Apples. Butter. A large jar of honey.

He grinned as he set it on the table. "From now on," he said, "this is how it will be."

Elisabetha touched the basket as though it might vanish. The children stared, wide-eyed.

"Eat now," Mathias said softly. And they did.

They ate until they were full. Kandid's face flushed with the shock of it. Martina licked honey from her fingers, her eyes shining.

In the months that followed, Kandid grew so quickly that neighbors remarked on it. His trousers crept up his ankles; his shirts strained at the buttons. By late autumn, he stood nearly a head taller, and people whispered that he would one day match his father's towering height.

Martina did not grow much taller in those months, but she filled out. Her eyes were bright, her mind quick, her spirit fierce. Her fate had been marked before she ever drew breath, but now she lived in a house where hunger no longer shaped her days.

The vow Mathias Stirnimann made before the tabernacle had taken root.

The hunger that had bound the household at last let them go.

And the Stirnimann family stepped, for the first time, into a life where fullness was possible.

Chapter Thirty-Two
The Library of Bertiswil

The library lived in the west barn, in the room Mathias had built for Elisabetha in the early years of their marriage. Her first husband's books filled the shelves—they were the best part of that chapter in her life. She did not remember Josef Moser with any fondness, but she remembered the books. Every last one of them. They had been her sole refuge during those lonely years. She had carried them to Ottorüthi not out of devotion to him, but because they were the tools of her mind, the proof that she belonged to a different world.

She often browsed the shelves of Latin classics, French fables, Greek primers, the histories and sermons and poetry. Elisabetha dusted them, repaired their bindings, and tended them as carefully as she tended her children. From the beginning of her second marriage, she had resolved that Josef's books would not remain her private inheritance. They were meant to be read, meant to be shared, meant to serve.

Mathias had approved of her plan from the beginning. "Let them be a blessing," he had said.

And then, when she learned that most of her neighbors could not read the books she offered, she began to teach them. First three *Knechte,* then a few farmers' wives, then a farmer's son or two. She taught anyone who appeared and asked to learn. The lessons were a quiet ministry and the library a place of learning as much as a house for books.

She taught her own children there, too. There was no proper school nearby—only a poorly trained teacher in a one room schoolhouse several kilometers away—and she would not send Kandid and Martina there. Under her instruction, they learned High German, French, Latin, and even a little Greek. Kandid absorbed things quickly, but like his father, his heart belonged to the land. Languages came easily to him, but so did the rhythms of soil and season. Martina was no less gifted, but her heart belonged to words—the shapes of them, the way they opened the world. In time, she developed an endless fascination with medicinal plants and cures, reading anything she could find on botany and *Heilkräuter.*

Over the years, the library's collection grew. Elisabetha added almanacs, books on healing herbs, various editions of the *Märchen* collected by the

Gebrüder Grimm, more volumes of Aesop's fables, travelogues, and the newly published novels of Jeremias Gotthelf, which the farmers devoured because they recognized themselves in the pages. But Josef's books remained the heart of the collection—the reason she taught, the reason she shared, the reason she believed knowledge could improve even the hardest life.

Her daughter grew up amongst those shelves. She learned her Latin from Josef's grammar, her French from his fables, her Greek from his worn primer. By the age of seven, she kept the library ledger in her neat printing, and by nine she could recommend books to patrons of their library almost as well as her mother.

Kandid's path diverged as he grew. By thirteen, he had grown almost to his father's shoulder, and he spent most days with Mathias—on the road, in the fields, at the cattle markets, or working alongside the *Knechte.* Uli, especially, took him under his wing, teaching him the rhythms of the land, the signs of weather, the ways of soil and seed. Kandid came home tired, sun-browned, and proud. He was becoming the man who would one day take over Ottorüthi.

Martina, meanwhile, drew closer to her mother. They were inseparable in the library, two quiet souls among the books. Elisabetha never neglected her household duties, and she taught them to her daughter just as her own mother had taught her. But when the chores and lessons were done, they slipped into the west barn, reading side by side in the quiet while the old timbers creaked softly overhead.

Mathias watched all of this with quiet pride. His *Knechte* had built the library's shelves and sealed it against the elements, but his wife had built the library. And their community was better for it.

He built his daughter a seat high in the apple tree in front of the *Bauernhaus*—a little platform with a rail, just wide enough for a girl and a book. It became her kingdom. She spent hours there, reading while the wind moved through the branches. Her mother smiled whenever she saw her daughter in that tree with a book; it reminded her of herself at that age in the pear tree on her parents' farm outside of Geltwil.

Martina was nine the afternoon a little girl wandered into the field by the Stirnimann farmhouse. She was reading *The Swiss Family Robinson* for the third time, legs dangling from her perch, when she saw movement below.

It was a child—six, perhaps—barefoot, thin, her dress filthy, her hair uncombed.

Martina called down, "*Grüezi!* Who might you be?"

The child startled and looked up into the branches.

"I'm Vreneli," she whispered.

"Are you lost, Vreneli?"

"*Nai.*"

A strange look crossed her face—fear, or guilt, or something Martina could not name—and then she turned and ran.

Martina told her parents about Vreneli that evening as the family gathered for *Znachtässä*.

Mathias listened, his expression tightening. "She must be one of the *Verdingchinder* on the Stadelmann farm."

He said nothing more, but the glance her parents exchanged told Martina that something might be wrong. The topic was closed for discussion.

At nine, Martina knew only vaguely what a *Verdingkind* was. Her parents knew too well. They had grown up in a Switzerland where orphaned, neglected, or simply unwanted children were "placed out" to work on farms—fed poorly, worked hard, often beaten, rarely loved. Some placements were decent. Most were not.

Kandid and Martina had been forbidden, since they were old enough to roam the property alone, to go near the Stadelmann land. It was far from Ottorüthi, beyond the fields and the rise of the hill, a place Mathias seldom saw and never visited. *Bauer* Stadelmann was a strange, solitary, childless man who hired no adult *Knechte*. He relied entirely on *Verdingkinder*. Their numbers changed constantly—older children left when their contracts ended, at fourteen or fifteen, and younger ones arrived in their place.

Mathias had never seen a girl as young as six among them.

He felt a coldness he could not name settle in his chest.

Perhaps Pater Birrer was right, he thought. Perhaps God was nudging him toward what he needed to do next—something he did not yet understand.

He would not pry.

He would not accuse without cause.

But he would watch.

And he would wait.

Chapter Thirty-Three
The Return of Vreneli

The afternoon had settled into that pale autumn stillness that made sound travel farther than it should. Even the chickens seemed subdued, scratching half-heartedly in the dust behind the house. Martina was sweeping the path between the barn library and the house, pushing aside the brittle curls of fallen leaves. The air smelled faintly of woodsmoke and the cool, earthy breath of the turning season.

She paused to rest her hands on the broom handle. From where she stood, she could see the bend in the road that curved around the alder shrubs. It was a familiar sight—the place where travelers first came into view, where a herd of cows first appeared, where deer sometimes cut across the field on their way to the stream.

But today something was different.

A small shape stood half-hidden in the shadow of the shrubs. At first Martina thought it might be a stray dog nosing at the ground, but then the figure straightened, and she saw the outline of thin arms, a narrow back, a head of tangled pale hair.

Her breath caught. She lowered the broom without meaning to.

"Vreneli?" she called, her voice barely above the hush of the wind.

The child jerked as if struck. She didn't run, but her whole body tightened, shoulders rising, chin dropping, as though bracing for a blow. Martina took a single step forward, palms open, the way one might approach a frightened animal.

"It's only me," she said softly. "You can come."

The girl's eyes flicked toward the house, then toward the fields, then back to the road behind her. She looked like someone checking for danger in every direction at once. Her dress hung crookedly from one shoulder, and her bare legs were streaked with dirt. She was thinner than Martina remembered—and she had been thin before.

The library door creaked open.

Elisabetha stepped out, brushing dust from her skirt. She had been inside for most of the afternoon, sorting through a stack of new books and repairing a torn page in the back of a child's catechism. The quiet of the library still clung to her—that particular stillness that came from being surrounded by books, by the soft weight of volumes waiting to be opened.

She heard the tremor in her daughter's voice before she saw the child. That was what made her look up.

"What is it?" she asked, but Martina didn't answer. She only nodded toward the gate.

Elisabetha followed her gaze—and stopped.

The small figure stood motionless, half-turned as if ready to flee. Even from a distance, Elisabetha could see the tension in her posture, the way her hands were clenched at her sides, the way her eyes darted about like a trapped bird's.

Elisabetha felt something tighten low in her chest. She stepped forward, but not too quickly. She knew better than to rush.

"Vreneli," she said, her voice low and even. "You're welcome here."

The child's eyes flicked to her and then away. She didn't speak. Her throat worked once, a small swallow.

Elisabetha took another step, then stopped. She lowered herself to a crouch so she wouldn't tower over the girl.

"No one will harm you," she said.

A gust of wind stirred the alder branches. The child flinched at the sound.

Martina glanced at her mother, her face tightening with worry. Elisabetha gave the smallest shake of her head. Let the child come in her own time.

"Are you hungry?" Elisabetha asked.

The girl hesitated. Then, almost imperceptibly, she nodded.

Elisabetha rose slowly. "Wait here," she said gently. "I have something to show you."

She turned and walked back toward the library, her steps measured, her breath steady. Inside, the air was cool and smelled faintly of ink and old paper. She crossed to the shelf where she kept the children's books—now a good-sized collection—and pulled down a brand new storybook of Biblical parables. The book had beautiful, multi-colored illustrations. Everyone who opened it lingered over the pictures.

She held it against her chest as she stepped back outside.

Vreneli had not moved. She watched Elisabetha with the wary stillness of a creature who had learned that safety was always temporary.

Elisabetha approached slowly, stopping a few paces away. She knelt again and opened the book so the child could see the pictures.

She didn't speak. She let the colorful illustrations do the work. The girl's breath hitched. She took a small step forward, then another, drawn by the image of what appeared to be a father running down the road, his arms opened wide, his son dressed in rags and barefoot.

Martina stood behind them, broom forgotten, her hands pressed together as if in prayer.

Elisabetha turned the page, her movements slow and deliberate. The child leaned closer, her eyes wide, her face softening with something like longing.

And then, in a voice so small it was almost a thought:

"*If only I had that.*"

The words hung in the cold air, fragile as frost.

Elisabetha felt them settle inside her like stones.

The librarian closed the storybook gently, as if the picture itself might shatter under too much force. She rose from her crouch, careful not to startle the child, and held the book against her chest.

"Come," she said. "Let's get you something to eat."

She didn't reach for the girl. She didn't offer her hand. She simply turned toward the house and walked slowly, giving Vreneli space to choose. Martina stayed where she was, broom forgotten, watching the child with a mixture of hope and fear.

For a moment, Vreneli didn't move. She stood rooted to the spot, her thin shoulders trembling under the weight of some invisible calculation. Then she took a step. And another. Her bare feet made no sound on the packed earth.

Martina let out a breath she hadn't realized she was holding.

Inside the house, the kitchen was warm. The smell of simmering barley soup lingered in the air, and the light from the small window fell across the table in a soft, slanted beam. Elisabetha moved with quiet purpose, opening the bread box, cutting a thick slice from the loaf she had baked that morning. She spread honey across it generously with the back of a spoon, the golden line catching the light. Then she poured out a cup of milk.

She placed a plate with the bread on the table together with the cup and stepped back.

Vreneli hovered in the doorway, her eyes darting around the kitchen at the stove, the table, the window, the shadows. She looked like someone expecting a trap.

"It's for you," Elisabetha said. "No one else will take it."

The girl approached the table slowly, her breath shallow. She climbed onto the bench and took the bread in both hands. She didn't say thank you. She didn't look up. She ate in quick, desperate bites, swallowing too fast, as if she feared the food might vanish if she didn't finish it in time.

Elisabetha stood near the stove, her hands clasped tightly in front of her. She and her children had experienced hunger, too. She had also witnessed the hunger of others—the kind that came from poverty, from hard winters, from families stretched too thin. But this was different. This was the hunger of someone who had learned that food—or the lack of it—was a weapon, a reward, a punishment.

She watched the child without pity, only with a deep, steady attention. Elisabetha had learned long ago that pity made people feel small. Attention made them feel seen.

When the bread was gone, she reached for the cup. After downing the milk in two large gulps, Vreneli wiped her mouth with the back of her hand. She glanced at the door, then at the window, then at the storybook still tucked under Elisabetha's arm.

"Would you like to see more?" Elisabetha asked.

The girl hesitated. Then she nodded.

The woman sat at the table and opened the book. She turned the pages slowly, letting the child see the bright illustrations—the shepherd finding the lost sheep, the widow lighting a lamp to search for her coin, and again, the father embracing the wayward son who had wandered far from home.

Vreneli leaned closer, her eyes fixed on the pictures. Her breathing slowed. For a moment, the tension in her shoulders eased.

Martina watched from across the room, her chest tightening. She had never seen a child so still, so focused. It was as if the pictures were a language she understood better than words.

Elisabetha turned another page. The feast. The ring. The robe. The father's arms around the son.

Vreneli's fingers hovered above the illustration, trembling slightly.

"*So schön,*" she whispered, barely audible.

Elisabetha didn't speak. She didn't touch the child. She simply let the moment settle between them, heavy yet fragile.

Outside, a cart rattled along the road, the driver calling to his oxen. The sound was distant, harmless—but to Vreneli it was something else entirely. Her body went rigid. Her eyes widened. She slid off the bench so quickly the storybook nearly fell from the table.

"Vreneli—" Martina began, but the child was already moving, her breath coming in sharp, panicked bursts.

Elisabetha rose, but she didn't reach for her. She knew better.

The girl bolted through the doorway, her small figure disappearing into the cold afternoon light. The sound of her footsteps faded down the path, swallowed by the wind.

Martina stood frozen, her hands pressed to her mouth. "She's terrified," she said. "Something is wrong."

Her mother closed the storybook gently, as if it were something fragile. She picked it up and held it against her chest, looking toward the bend in the road where the child had vanished.

"*Ja*," she said quietly. "I know."

For a long moment after Vreneli vanished down the path, neither Elisabetha nor her daughter moved. The kitchen felt suddenly too still, the air too warm, as if the room itself were holding its breath. Outside, the wind rattled the bare branches of the pear tree, and a loose shutter tapped against the side of the house with a hollow, rhythmic sound.

The nine-year-old Martina lowered her hands from her mouth. "She looked…wrong," she said. "Not just hungry. Not just scared. Wrong."

Elisabetha didn't answer right away. She smoothed her hand over the worn cover of the storybook she still held against her body. The gesture was slow, almost ceremonial, as though she were taking comfort in its familiar feel.

"She's been coming around more often," Martina said. "First just watching from the road. Then closer. Today she came all the way to the gate."

Elisabetha nodded. "Children don't come back to a place unless something in them knows it's safe."

"She must be really afraid of something," Martina said quietly.

Elisabetha looked toward the window. The bend in the road was empty now, the alder shrubs swaying in the wind. She imagined the child running, breath sharp, feet stinging against the cold ground. She imagined the fear that drove her—a fear so deep it lived in her bones.

She felt a slow, steady anger rise in her chest. Not the hot, reckless kind, but the cold, clear kind that sharpened thought and steadied her hands.

"Sit," Elisabetha told her daughter in a gentle voice. "You're shaking."

Martina sank onto the bench. She was only nine, but in that moment she looked younger, her face pale, her eyes wide with something like guilt.

"I should have gone after her," she said. "I should have—"

"No," Elisabetha said. "Chasing her would have frightened her more."

Martina swallowed hard. "She's so small."

"Yes."

"And she's alone."

Elisabetha hesitated. "Not entirely."

Martina looked up sharply. "What do you mean?"

"She has companions," Elisabetha said. "Others in the same situation as she is. The *Verdingchinder* on that farm…they cling to each other. I've seen it before. They try to look out for one another as best they can—but they are only children."

Martina's brow furrowed. "Why do you think she is the only one who comes, Mama?"

Elisabetha didn't answer. She didn't know. Or perhaps she did, but the knowing was too heavy to speak aloud.

She crossed to the window and rested her hand on the sill. The chill from the glass seeped into her skin. Outside, the light was fading, the sky turning the color of pewter. Evening would come soon, and with it the lengthening autumn dark.

"She'll come back," Elisabetha said. "Not today. But soon."

"How do you know?"

She paused. "Because she has need."

Martina stared at the table. "She said…*if only I had that.*"

Her mother closed her eyes for a moment. The words echoed in her mind as well, soft and devastating.

"I'm not even sure she was talking about the father in the parable," she said. "Not the man in the picture," Elisabetha said suddenly.

"Then what?"

"The welcome. The arms open. The running toward, not away. The love."

Martina's throat tightened. "She's never had that."

"*Nai.*"

The wind picked up outside, carrying with it the faint sound of a distant dog barking. The house creaked softly, settling into the cold.

Martina looked up, her eyes older than her years. "Do you think someone is hurting her?"

Elisabetha didn't answer right away. She kept her gaze on the bend in the road, the place where the child had stood, trembling and thin and hungry.

"I think," she said slowly, "that something is happening on that farm. Something we don't know yet."

Martina's voice was barely a whisper. "Something bad."

"*Ja.* I will talk to Papa about it. He will know what is to be done."

A long silence settled between them. Not empty—heavy. Full of the things they didn't yet have words for.

Finally, Elisabetha turned from the window. She was still holding the storybook.

"Put on your shawl," she said to her daughter. "We'll walk to the library. I want to put this back where it belongs."

Martina frowned. "Why now?"

"Because she'll come looking for it," Elisabetha said with a shrug. "And I want it to be there when she does."

They stepped outside into the cold. The sky had darkened to a deep, bruised blue, and the first stars were beginning to appear. The path between the house and the library was quiet, the air sharp against their cheeks.

As they walked, Martina glanced toward the road again, as if expecting the small figure to reappear. But the bend was empty, the shrubs still.

Inside the library, the air was cool and smelled faintly of dust and ink. Elisabetha crossed to the children's shelf and slid the storybook back into its place. She rested her fingers on the spine for a moment, then let her hand fall.

"She'll come back," she said again, more to herself than to Martina.

Martina nodded, though her eyes were troubled. "And when she does?"

Elisabetha looked at the shelf, at the quiet rows of books waiting in the dim light.

"When she does," she said, "we'll be ready." The room felt different now—it was not just a place of books, but a place of safety that had been chosen by a frightened child as a point of return.

Martina wrapped her shawl tighter around her shoulders. "Do you think she'll come again tomorrow?"

"Not tomorrow," Elisabetha said. "But soon."

"How can you be sure?"

Elisabetha didn't answer right away. She walked to the window and looked out at the darkening yard. The last of the daylight clung to the horizon, a thin line of silver fading into blue. The path between the house and the road was empty, but she could almost see the small figure standing there—thin, trembling, eyes darting like a creature who had learned to expect pain.

"She came because she needed something—a place where she isn't afraid." Elisabetha said.

The words hung in the air, quiet and heavy.

Elisabetha closed the library door and latched it. The click of the latch echoed softly in the stillness. The mother and daughter walked back toward the house, their footsteps muffled by the cold earth. The sky had now deepened to a dark indigo, and the stars were sharp and bright above the fields. A thin crescent moon hung low, pale as bone.

Inside, the fire in the kitchen stove had burned low. Elisabetha added a small log and watched the flames catch. The warmth spread slowly, pushing back the chill that had settled in her bones. Martina sat at the table, her hands wrapped around a mug of warm milk. She stared into it as if it might offer answers.

"I keep thinking about the way she ate," she said. "Like she didn't know if she'd get another chance."

Elisabetha nodded. "Children learn what the world teaches them."

"But she's just a little girl."

"*Ja. Sicher.*"

Martina looked up, her eyes shining with something like anger. "Why doesn't anyone stop it? Why doesn't anyone see?"

Elisabetha sat across from her daughter. "People see what they want to see. And they look away from what frightens them."

Martina's jaw tightened. "But you didn't look away."

Elisabetha didn't respond. She watched the flames curl around the wood. She thought of the child's whisper—*if only I had that*—and felt it settle deeper inside her, a quiet, haunting ache.

After a long silence, Martina spoke again. "Do you think the others are like her? The other children on that farm?"

Elisabetha's breath caught. She did not know these children, but when she lived on her parents' farm in Aargau, she had seen glimpses of others—the way the eldest boys stood between the younger ones, the way the girls' eyes darted as if they were cornered animals, the way they flinched at sudden sounds. She had seen enough to know that fear was not an exception among *Verdingkinder*. It was the rule.

"I think," she said slowly, "that whatever is happening to her is not happening to her alone."

Martina shivered. "Then we must do something, Mama."

"We will certainly try, *Tochter*," Elisabetha said. "But not yet. Not until we understand more."

Martina nodded, though her hands trembled around the mug.

The fire crackled softly. Outside, the wind picked up, rattling the shutters. The house felt both sheltering and fragile, as if the walls themselves understood the weight of what had entered them that day.

Elisabetha rose and went to the window. Mathias and Kandid would be home soon. She looked out at the dark path, the bend in the road hidden now in shadow. She imagined Vreneli running, breath sharp, feet cold, fear driving her like a whip.

"She'll come back soon," Elisabetha repeated again, her voice barely above a whisper.

Martina joined her at the window.

Elisabetha rested a hand on her daughter's shoulder. "When she does," she said, "we'll be here. And we'll listen."

The wind sighed against the house. And somewhere beyond the bend in the road, a small girl trudged alone through the dark, bearing a secret that would soon break open the quiet of Bertiswil.

Chapter Thirty-Four
Intervention

The house had settled into its nighttime stillness, the kind that came only after the children were asleep and the last chores were done. The fire in the kitchen stove had burned low, leaving a faint orange glow that pulsed against the walls like a slow heartbeat. The wooden floorboards creaked softly as the house cooled, the old timber shifting into its familiar nighttime posture.

Elisabetha moved quietly through the bedroom, folding her shawl and placing it on the chest at the foot of the bed. Her hands were steady, but her mind was not. The image of the small girl—thin, trembling, eyes darting like a hunted creature—kept rising before her, unbidden and sharp.

Mathias was washing at the basin, his sleeves rolled to his elbows, the lamplight catching the lines at the corners of his eyes. He glanced at his wife once, then again, sensing the tension in her posture.

"You're especially quiet tonight," he said, drying his hands on a towel.

Elisabetha hesitated. She had been waiting for this moment, waiting for the children to be asleep, waiting for the house to be still enough to hold the weight of what she needed to say.

"We had a visitor today," she said softly.

Mathias paused, the towel still in his hands. "A visitor?"

"A child, about six years old."

He turned fully toward her now, his expression sharpening. "Which child?"

"Her name is Vreneli. She is one of Stadelmann's *Verdingchinder*—the one Martina has seen here before."

A long silence followed. Outside, the wind brushed against the shutters, a thin, restless sound.

Mathias finally set the hand towel aside. "Tell me."

Elisabetha drew a slow breath. "She came to the gate first. She looked…wrong, Mathias. Not just hungry. Not just frightened. Wrong in a way that sits in the bones."

He listened without interrupting, his face unreadable but intent.

"She wouldn't come at first. She stood there like a creature expecting a blow. But she was hungry. So I brought her inside. Gave her bread with honey. Milk. She ate as if she didn't know if she'd ever eat again."

Mathias's jaw tightened, but he said nothing.

"Martina saw it, too," Elisabetha continued. "She's only nine, but even she felt it. She said something is wrong at that farm."

Mathias exhaled slowly, a sound that was almost a sigh. "Martina is wise for her years. Too wise sometimes."

"She's right," Elisabetha said. "I feel it as surely as I feel the cold in my hands."

Mathias sat on the edge of the bed, elbows on his knees, hands clasped loosely. He stared at the floorboards for a long moment, thinking. When he finally spoke, his voice was low.

"Did the girl say anything?"

Elisabetha nodded. "She whispered, '*If only I had that.*' She was looking at a picture of the father running to embrace the prodigal son."

Mathias closed his eyes briefly, as if absorbing a blow. "And then?"

"She panicked when a cart passed on the road. Ran off. As if she expected someone to come for her."

Another silence settled between them, heavier this time.

Mathias rubbed a hand over his face. "The Stadelmann farm has always been…difficult. The old man is secretive. Hard. People avoid crossing him."

"I know," Elisabetha said. "But this is different. This is fear. And she was ragged and filthy. Not to mention ravenous."

Mathias looked up at her, and in his eyes she saw the shift—the moment when her husband became not just a father and farmer, but the *Friedensrichter*, the man responsible for the quiet order of their hamlet.

"What exactly did you see?" he asked. "Every detail."

She told him. Her appearance. The trembling. The flinching. The way the girl's eyes scanned every doorway. The way she ate. The way she ran.

Mathias listened with the stillness of a man weighing each word, each implication.

When she finished, he sat back, hands resting on his thighs. "I'll think on it," he said quietly. "And I'll ask a few questions. Quietly. No one needs to know yet."

Elisabetha nodded, though her heart was still tight. "I don't want to frighten those children more—or cause even more trouble for them."

"I won't," he said. "But if something is happening on that farm, I need to find out."

He reached for the lamp, lowering the wick until the flame dimmed to a soft glow. The room fell into shadow, the kind that made the night feel deeper, closer.

As they lay down together, Elisabetha stared at the ceiling, listening to the wind. Mathias's breathing was steady beside her, but she knew he was awake, thinking.

Both of them slept only fitfully.

The next morning dawned pale and cold, the kind of light that made the frost on the grass look like a thin layer of ground glass. Elisabetha rose early, as she always did, but her movements were slower, her thoughts still heavy from the night before. She fed the kitchen stove and set water to boil. The house was quiet except for the soft breathing of the children upstairs and the occasional creak of the rafters.

Martina came down the stairs rubbing her eyes, her hair pulled into two uneven braids she had made herself. She paused at the bottom step, looking toward the window as if expecting to see a small figure standing there.

"She won't come this early. She will have chores to do," Elisabetha said gently.

Martina nodded, though her gaze lingered on the road. "I know. I just…keep thinking about her."

"So do I."

They ate breakfast quietly. Even the clatter of spoons against bowls seemed too loud for the morning. When Mathias left for the day, he paused at the door, his hand resting on the frame.

"I'll ask around," he said.

Elisabetha nodded. "Be careful."

He gave a faint smile. "I always am."

But she saw the tension in his shoulders as he walked away, the way he glanced toward the Stadelmann land before turning down the path.

The days that followed were marked by a strange kind of waiting. Not the impatient kind, but the heavy, watchful kind.

Martina checked the road every time she passed the window. She lingered near the gate when she fetched water. She swept the path between the house and the barn library twice a day, though it hardly needed it.

Elisabetha pretended not to notice, but she did. She noticed everything.

She kept the library tidy, the shelves in perfect order, the storybook of parables placed where small hands could find it easily. She left the door unlatched during the day, just in case.

Sometimes she stood in the doorway, looking out at the bend in the road where the alder shrubs grew thick. The wind moved through them with a soft rustling sound, like whispers she couldn't quite make out.

But the road remained empty.

On the third day, the weather shifted. A cold wind swept down from the hills, carrying with it the smell of damp earth and distant rain. Clouds gathered low and heavy, turning the afternoon light to a muted gray.

Martina was in the barn library, shelf reading—a task she invented for herself, though her mother didn't correct her. The girl's movements were restless, her fingers trailing against the spines as if trying to keep her worry from spilling out.

"Mama," she said suddenly, "what if she doesn't come back?"

Elisabetha looked up from the books she was cataloguing. "She will."

"How do you know?"

"Because she came once. And because she needs something she hasn't found yet."

Martina swallowed, her eyes shining. "I hate waiting."

"I know," Elisabetha said softly. "But waiting is a part of life."

Martina didn't answer. She went to the door, opened it, and began to stare at the road.

Elisabetha watched her daughter's small, tense form and felt a familiar ache rise in her chest. Children should not have to carry this kind of worry. But the world did not spare them.

Later that afternoon, as the light began its slow fade into the bruised blue of early evening, Elisabetha stepped outside to gather the last of the laundry from the line. The wind tugged at the sheets, snapping them like sails. She worked quickly, her fingers stiff from the cold.

When she turned toward the house, she saw Martina standing in the doorway of the barn library, her posture suddenly rigid.

"Mama," she whispered. "Look."

Elisabetha followed her gaze.

A small figure stood at the bend in the road.

Thin. Still. Watching.

Vreneli.

She looked even smaller than before, her dress a little askew, her hair tangled by the wind. She hesitated at the gate, her eyes darting toward the house, the fields, the road behind her.

Elisabetha felt her breath catch.

"Go inside," she told Martina gently. "I'll bring her in."

But Martina didn't move. She stood rooted to the spot, her hands pressed together as if in prayer.

Elisabetha dropped her laundry basket. She walked slowly toward the gate, her steps measured, her palms open.

"Vreneli," she said softly. "You're welcome here."

The child flinched at the sound of her name, but she didn't run. She took a small step forward, then another, drawn by something she couldn't name.

Elisabetha opened the gate.

"Come," she said. "It's cold. We have warmth inside."

Vreneli hesitated only a moment longer before slipping through the gate like a shadow.

Elisabetha led her toward the barn library, where Martina waited with wide, hopeful eyes.

The child stepped inside, her gaze sweeping the room, lingering on the shelves of books, the desk, chairs, and benches.

The library felt as if something had settled back into place. And then—just as the fragile peace began to settle—footsteps pounded outside.

Fast. Urgent. Panicked.

Martina gasped.

Elisabetha turned toward the door.

Someone was coming.

The footsteps grew louder—quick, uneven, the sound of someone running hard over cold ground. Elisabetha felt the air in the library tense. Martina's hands flew to her mouth. Even Vreneli, who had been inching toward the storybook shelf, froze where she stood, her thin shoulders rising as if bracing for a blow.

The door burst open.

A boy stood in the doorway, panting, his cheeks flushed from the cold and the run. He was older than Vreneli by perhaps four years—thin, wiry, his clothes too small and patched in places. His hair stuck to his forehead with sweat, and his eyes were wide with a fear that seemed to swallow the room.

He barely looked at Elisabetha and Martina. He didn't greet them. His gaze locked immediately on the small girl beside the table.

"*Vreneli!*" he hissed, his voice sharp with panic. "What are you doing? We're going to be in trouble—big trouble!"

The girl flinched as if struck. She took a step back, but the boy had already crossed the room in three quick strides. He grabbed her wrist with the desperate grip of someone trying to save another from falling off a cliff.

"Not yet, Kobi!" she cried out.

"You're supposed to be in the east field," he said, breathless. "Picking up stones. He said it has to be done before supper or there'll be hell to pay."

Vreneli's lips parted, but no sound came out.

"And the turnips," the boy named Kobi went on, his voice rising. "You didn't finish the row. I had to do half of it for you this morning, and he still said it wasn't good enough."

Elisabetha felt something cold settle in her stomach.

Kobi's grip tightened. "And the eggs—you didn't bring the eggs in. He already checked the coop. He's going to know you ran off again."

Again. The word struck like a stone.

Vreneli's eyes filled with tears. She shook her head, a tiny, frantic motion.

"I just wanted—" she whispered.

"No!" Kobi cut her off, his voice cracking. "You can't! You know that. If he finds out you're here—if he sees you're gone—he'll beat us both."

Martina gasped, a small, strangled sound.

Elisabetha stepped forward, her voice steady. "Kobi," she said gently. "She's not in trouble here. She's safe."

But the boy recoiled as if her words were dangerous. He shook his head hard, eyes darting toward the open door, toward the road, toward the world beyond the library walls.

"We are *not* safe," he said, barely audible. "Not there. Not here. Not anywhere."

He tugged at Vreneli's arm. "Come on. We have to go. Now."

Vreneli hesitated—just for a heartbeat. Her gaze flicked to the storybook on the shelf, the one with the father running toward the son. Her fingers twitched, as if reaching for something she couldn't name.

Then Kobi pulled again, harder this time, and the moment broke.

"Vreneli," he whispered urgently, "*please*."

The girl let out a small, wounded sound—half sob, half breath—and allowed herself to be led.

They ran.

Out the door.

Down the path.

Toward the bend in the road where the alder shrubs shivered in the wind.

The door swung shut behind them with a hollow thud that echoed through the library like the closing of a vault.

For a long moment, no one moved.

Martina stood rigid, her hands trembling. "Mama," she whispered, "did you hear what he said?"

Elisabetha couldn't speak. Her throat felt tight, her breath shallow. She stared at the door, at the empty space where the children had been, at the dust still settling in the air.

She had suspected.

She had feared.

But now—now she had heard it with her own ears.

The truth was no longer a shadow.

It had a voice.

A child's voice, thin and terrified.

Something was happening on that farm.

Something cruel.

Something that could no longer be ignored.

"Come," she said softly to Martina. "Let's go back to the house."

Her voice was calm, but her heart was pounding.

Tonight, she would tell Mathias everything.

And this time, he would not wait.

The wind had picked up by the time Elisabetha and Martina reached the house, rattling the shutters and carrying the sharp scent of oncoming rain. The sky had darkened to a deep, sullen gray, and the first drops began to patter against the roof as they stepped inside.

Martina's face was pale, her eyes wide and unfocused. She clutched the edge of her shawl as if holding herself together.

"Mama," she whispered, "he said they'd be beaten."

Elisabetha closed the door behind them, leaning against it for a moment as she gathered her breath. The house felt too warm, too still, as if the walls themselves were listening.

"I know," she said softly.

"Why would he say that? Why would he—"

"Because it's true. Because he's afraid," Elisabetha murmured. "And because fear teaches children to speak truths they would never dare say otherwise. Unfortunately, Martina, it is the fate of many children to endure beatings at the hands of their elders in the name of discipline," Elisabetha said grimly. "There is no law against beating a child, unless the force is deemed excessive."

Martina swallowed hard. "*Mama. Can't we help them?*"

"We will try," Elisabetha said, though the words felt heavy on her tongue. "But we must be careful. And we must be wise."

She crossed to the stove and added a small log, watching the flames catch and flare. The firelight flickered across the kitchen, casting shadows that stretched and shrank against the walls.

Martina stood beside her mother, trembling. "Do you think they're all right?"

Elisabetha didn't answer immediately. She thought of Kobi's face—flushed, frantic, eyes darting like a cornered animal. She thought of the way he had grabbed Vreneli's wrist, not in anger but in desperation. She thought of the chores he had listed, each one a small stone in the load the child carried. "I think," she said slowly, "that they are doing what they must to survive."

Martina's eyes filled with tears. "That's not fair."

"No," Elisabetha said. "It isn't."

They stood in silence for a long moment, listening to the wind and the soft crackle of the fire.

The house felt smaller than usual, as if the weight of what they had witnessed pressed inward from all sides.

Mathias returned just after dusk with Kandid beside him, their coats damp from the rain, their boots thick with mud. When he opened the door, a gust of cold air swept in ahead of them. They stepped onto the threshold, stamping off what they could, then bent to unlace their boots. Both father and son left them by the door and shrugged out of their wet coats, hanging them on the pegs to drip.

Only then did Mathias cross into the room in his stockinged feet. He paused, taking in the stillness, and sensed at once that something was wrong.

"What happened?" he asked quietly.

Elisabetha met his gaze. "Sit," she said. "There is something you need to hear."

He pulled out a chair and sat, his posture straight, his expression alert. Martina hovered near the stove, her hands twisting her skirt. Kandid stood close to his sister, his hand resting on her shoulder.

Elisabetha sat across from her husband. For a moment, she simply looked at him—at the man she had built a life with, the man who carried the quiet authority of the *Friedensrichter* even in the way he rested his hands on the table.

Then she told him.

She told him about Vreneli's return.

About the way the child had stood at the gate, trembling.

About the way she had relaxed, just barely, in the warmth of the library.

About the moment the door burst open.

About the boy named Kobi and his breathless panic.

About the chores—picking up stones from the east field, the unfinished turnip row, the eggs left uncollected.

About the word *again.*

About the threat of a beating.

About the way the children had run. Mathias listened without interrupting, his face growing more grave with each detail. When she finished, he sat back slowly, his jaw tight.

"Did he say anything else?" he asked.

"No," Elisabetha said. "He barely looked at us. He was too afraid."

Mathias nodded once, a small, controlled motion. "And Vreneli?"

"She barely said a word. Not after he came. She just ran off with him."

Martina stepped forward, her voice trembling. "Papa, he's hurting them. He must be."

Mathias looked at his daughter, and his expression softened. "I believe you," he said gently.

He turned back to Elisabetha. "This is no longer mere suspicion."

"No," she said. "It isn't."

Mathias exhaled slowly, his breath steady but heavy. "Stadelmann has always been a strange man. But this—this is something else."

Elisabetha nodded. "What will you do?"

He didn't answer right away. He stared at the table, his fingers tapping once against the wood—a small, thoughtful gesture she had seen many times before, usually when he was weighing a difficult judgment.

"I will speak to a few people," he said finally. "Quietly. Those who have worked near the Stadelmann land. Those who might have seen something."

"And then?" Elisabetha asked.

"And then," he said, "I will go to the farm myself."

Martina sighed with relief. Mathias's voice remained calm. "I won't go to accuse. I will go to observe. To ask questions. To make it clear that someone is paying attention."

Elisabetha felt a chill run through her. The wind howled outside, rattling the shutters. The fire glowed softly in the stove.

The giant of a man rose and placed one of his large hands on his wife's shoulder. "You did right," he said quietly. "Both of you."

But his eyes were troubled.

After supper, the house settled into its usual rhythms, but the air felt different—charged, expectant, as if the walls themselves were listening for footsteps on the road. At bedtime, Martina lingered at the doorway of her room, her hand gripping the frame.

"Mama," she whispered, "what if they get hurt because they came here?"

Elisabetha brushed a strand of hair from her daughter's forehead. "We must pray that it does not happen. And hope for the best."

"But Kobi said—"

"I know what he said." Elisabetha's voice softened.

She kissed her daughter's cheek and watched her climb into bed, small and tense beneath the quilt. When she closed the door, the hallway felt colder.

Downstairs, Mathias sat at the table, the lamplight casting a warm circle around him. His *Amtsbuch* lay open, but he wasn't writing. He stared at it as if the pages before him might offer answers.

Elisabetha joined him, her hands folded in her lap. For a moment, neither spoke. The only sounds were the wind pressing against the shutters and the faint crackle of the fire.

Finally, Mathias closed the book.

"I didn't want to say this in front of our daughter, but I spoke with Jakob Huber today," he said quietly. "He works the field that borders the Stadelmann land."

Elisabetha's breath caught. "And?"

Mathias hesitated. "He said he's seen the children out before dawn. Working long after dark. He said the old man keeps them close. Too close."

Elisabetha felt a chill run through her. "Did he say anything else?"

Mathias nodded slowly. "He said he's heard shouting. And several times—crying."

The room seemed to shrink around them.

"Why didn't he say anything?" Elisabetha whispered.

Mathias's expression tightened. "Because people don't want trouble with Stadelmann. Because they think it's not their place. Because it is not against the law to make children work in Switzerland—nor is it against the law to shout at them or discipline them physically. Because they tell themselves it is not their concern."

Elisabetha looked at him, her eyes steady. "But it is."

Mathias held her gaze, something hardening inside him. "Yes. It is."

He reached across the table and took her hand. His grip was warm, steady, grounding. "You did right to try to help that child."

Elisabetha looked down at their joined hands. "I wish we could do more."

"We will," Mathias said. "One step at a time."

Later, when the lamps were extinguished and the house lay in darkness, Elisabetha stood at the bedroom window, looking out at the faint outline of the road. The moon had risen, thin and pale, casting a silver sheen across the fields. The alder shrubs at the bend swayed in the wind, their branches whispering secrets she could not hear.

Somewhere out there, children were working in the cold.

Somewhere out there, fear ruled a household.

Somewhere out there, small children carried burdens too heavy for their thin shoulders.

Elisabetha pressed her hand against the cold glass.

"She'll come back," she murmured to the night. "And when she does, we'll be here."

Behind her, Mathias shifted in bed, the weight of his coming task settling into his bones.

Outside, the wind sighed through the fields, carrying with it the faintest echo of footsteps—real or imagined, she could not tell.

But she knew one thing with certainty: the innocence of Bertiswil was ending.

And nothing would ever be the same again.

Chapter Thirty-Five
Violation

The morning broke cold and colorless, the kind of light that flattened the fields and deepened every furrow. Mathias dressed in silence, each movement deliberate. Elisabetha watched from the doorway, her shawl tight around her shoulders.

"You don't have to go alone," she said.

"I do. If I bring anyone else, it becomes a spectacle. And he'll shut his doors even tighter."

She nodded, fingers twisting the fringe of her shawl.

Outside, the cold bit at his cheeks. As he crossed the yard, he passed the barn library. The door stood slightly ajar, a sliver of warm light spilling onto the frost-hardened ground. He paused. He thought of the girl who had been trembling inside. The boy bursting in, breathless. Elisabetha's voice breaking as she told him what she'd seen. The library felt changed now, marked by what it had witnessed.

Mathias drew a slow breath and continued down the path.

The Stadelmann farm sat at the edge of the hamlet like a raw wound—buildings sagging, the yard cluttered with broken tools and rusted metal, fields worn thin from overuse. Smoke rose from the chimney in a thin, reluctant line.

Two children moved near the barn, hauling a heavy milk bucket between them. Thin. Dirty. Clothes patched and ragged. They didn't look up. They didn't speak. Their eyes stayed fixed on the ground.

Mathias's jaw tightened.

He stopped a few paces away. "*Grüezi*," he said brightly.

Neither child responded. One flinched.

The farmhouse door slammed open.

Kaspar Stadelmann stepped out, broad-shouldered beneath a stained work shirt, his face set in a hard scowl. His boots struck the ground in a heavy rhythm as he approached Mathias.

"What do you want?" he barked. "I've got work to do."

"*Guete Morge*, *Herr* Stadelmann," Mathias said evenly. "I'm here as *Friedensrichter*."

"This is my land. You've no business here."

"I do when there are concerns about the welfare of children."

A flicker crossed the man's face—quick, sharp.

"Concerns?" he spat. "Old women gossip too much."

Mathias gestured toward the children. "They look underfed. Exhausted. Working before dawn and after dark."

"They work because they eat," Stadelmann snapped. "That's how it is."

"I've heard you're beating them."

The yard went still.

The children froze.

Stadelmann's face darkened. "And what of it? A beating never hurt a child."

"Until it crosses a line."

"It's discipline. None of your concern."

"It is when a child runs from your farm in fear. When she trembles at the sound of a cart. When she eats as if she hasn't been fed in days."

"You're meddling where you shouldn't, Stirnimann."

"And you're harming the children entrusted to you."

Stadelmann stepped closer, close enough that Mathias could smell sweat and old tobacco. "Leave. Now. Before I make you."

Mathias didn't move. He didn't flinch. "I will leave. But this is not finished."

"It's finished when I say it is."

Mathias turned—not out of fear, but because nothing more could be gained that day. As he walked away, he glanced once more at the children. One risked a quick look up—a flicker of something like hope, or fear—before dropping his gaze again.

The weight of that look settled deep in Mathias's chest.

Something was wrong here. Worse than he'd feared.

He quickened his pace on the road, unaware that before the day was over, the truth would come to his doorstep in a way he could never have imagined.

By afternoon, the light had thinned to a pale, brittle gold. Martina finished her chores, humming softly as she carried a basket of kindling. She paused at the gate.

Something moved on the path.

A small figure. Slow. Unsteady.

"Vreneli? *Vreneli!*"

The girl didn't answer. She drifted forward like someone walking in a trance, her face pale beneath the dirt, her dress torn at the hem. A dark stain marked the skirt.

Blood.

The basket slipped from Martina's hands.

"Vreneli!" she cried out again, running toward her.

The girl swayed. Martina caught her under the arms, shocked by how light she was, how limp. The child's head fell against her shoulder, her breath shallow and uneven. "Help!" Martina croaked, her voice breaking. "Please…someone help!"

She half-carried, half-dragged the girl toward the house. The door flew open—her mother had heard the cry.

"Martina? What—"

Then she saw the child. Elisabetha's face drained of color. She swept Vreneli into her arms with a strength born of fear.

"Fetch the *Knecht*," she said, low and urgent. "Now."

Martina ran.

Elisabetha carried the girl inside and laid her on the kitchen table. Vreneli whimpered at the touch of the wood, curling in on herself. Her hands clutched at Elisabetha's sleeve, fingers trembling.

"*Shh*," Elisabetha murmured, brushing hair from her forehead. "You're safe."

The girl's lips moved.

"*The…book…*"

Elisabetha leaned closer. "What, child?"

"*The…father…*"

A breath. A shiver.

"*The picture…*"

Her voice faded.

Something inside Elisabetha cracked. The parable picture in the book. The father running to embrace the lost child. Even in terror, the girl reached for the only place she'd felt a flicker of safety.

The *Knecht* burst through the door, breathless. "*Frau* Stirnimann?"

"Find Uli. Tell him to ride for the doctor in Rothenburg. As fast as he can."

He nodded and ran.

The girl's breath hitched, her small body shaking.

Martina returned, pale and wide-eyed. "*Mama…what happened to her?*"

Elisabetha couldn't answer. Not in words a child could bear.

"Bring blankets," she said. "Warm ones."

Martina ran again.

Elisabetha felt the fragile rise and fall of Vreneli's breath, the faint warmth of her skin.

Outside, hooves struck the ground—Uli riding hard.

Inside, the world narrowed to the child on the kitchen table.

❦

Uli returned just after dusk, his horse lathered and trembling. The doctor from Rothenburg rode behind him, coat flapping, face set in a grim line. He dismounted before the horse had fully stopped.

"Where is the child?" he asked tersely.

Martina led him inside.

The kitchen was warm. Blankets were piled around Vreneli. Her breath was shallow, her eyes fluttering open and closed as if the world were too heavy to hold.

The doctor washed his hands at the basin, the water turning cloudy with road dust.

"I will need space," he said.

"I'm not leaving her," Elisabetha replied.

He didn't argue.

He approached the table, his movements careful. "*Liebes Meiteli,*" he said gently, "I must examine you. It will not take long."

Vreneli whimpered, shrinking back. One hand gripped Elisabetha's sleeve; the other clutched at her skirt, trying to hold it down.

"I'm here," Elisabetha whispered. "I won't go."

The girl's fingers tightened.

He worked quickly and gently.

Silence settled—broken only by the girl's sharp, involuntary breaths. Elisabetha kept her eyes on Vreneli's face, murmuring soft reassurances she knew could not reach the depth of the child's pain. But it was the only thing she knew how to do.

At one point, Vreneli gasped and buried her face against Elisabetha's arm. She stroked the girl's hair, her own breath unsteady.

When it was over, the doctor stepped back, his expression carved from stone. Elisabetha thought she saw tears in his eyes.

She stayed where she was, shielding the child with her body.

"*Frau* Stirnimann," the doctor said quietly. "May I speak with you?"

"I cannot leave her."

He nodded. "Then I will speak here."

He leaned close and whispered, though even a whisper could not blunt the ugliness of the truth.

"She has been violated. Not once. Repeatedly."

The world tilted, but Elisabetha did not let go of Vreneli's hand.

"There are injuries consistent with ongoing assault," he continued. "Days, perhaps weeks. Possibly longer."

Elisabetha closed her eyes. "*She can't be more than six.*"

"I know," he said softly.

A long silence followed, broken only by the child's uneven breaths.

"Will she live?" Elisabetha asked.

"Yes," the doctor said. "Physically, she will recover. But as for the rest…" He shook his head. "She will need care. Safety. Stability. And she must not be returned to that farm."

"She won't be," Elisabetha said, her voice low and fierce.

The doctor closed his notebook. "I'll file a report with the authorities. This cannot be ignored."

"No," Elisabetha whispered. "It cannot."

She bowed her head, covering her mouth with her hand. A tear slipped down her cheek.

Vreneli stirred, her fingers tightening around Elisabetha's.

"*Frau…?*" she whispered.

"I'm here," Elisabetha murmured.

She did not let go.

The air in the kitchen felt close. The child shifted on the table, trying to find a position that didn't hurt.

Footsteps sounded at the door—heavy, familiar. Mathias appeared, pale, eyes searching his wife's. She looked at him, and he understood without a word. His face crumpled—not with tears, but with something deeper.

Horror. Sorrow. Guilt.

He leaned against the wall, covering his eyes. "I should have gone sooner," he said, voice raw. "I should have known."

"You couldn't have," Elisabetha said.

"I felt it," he whispered. "And I waited."

She touched his arm. "We know now. And we will act."

He lowered his hand, resolve hardening in his expression.

Martina had slipped away while the adults spoke in low, urgent voices. She moved down the hallway like someone walking through a dream. She didn't want to see the doctor's grave face or her father's hollow eyes.

She needed somewhere quiet.

Her steps carried her outside to the barn library. The door creaked softly as she pushed it open. She lit the gas lamp. Dust motes drifted in the air like tiny aimless stars.

Martina sat at the desk, folding her hands in her lap. She didn't know exactly what had happened. But she knew enough: something terrible had been done to the small girl who had once stood trembling in this room. Something that made her bleed. Something that emptied her eyes.

Martina pressed her palms together.

"*Lieber Gott*, please let Vreneli be all right," she whispered.

The wind brushed against the barn walls, a soft, mournful sound.

Inside the house, the doctor packed his case. He spoke quietly with Elisabetha, giving instructions for care and what to watch for in the coming days. His voice was steady, but his eyes carried the weight of what he had seen. Then he turned to the *Friedensrichter:* all of the *Verdingkinder* must be removed from Stadelmann's farm as soon as arrangements could be made, and the man brought to justice.

The house felt hollow after he left. Elisabetha stood in the kitchen doorway, watching the rise and fall of Vreneli's breath beneath the blankets. She closed her eyes and let herself feel it—the horror, the helplessness, the fierce protectiveness. When she opened them again, the room steadied.

She would not let this child be lost.

Mathias stood beside the table, his hands braced on the edge. The lamplight cast a soft glow over the child's face, illuminating the faint smudges of dirt, the crease between her brows that did not ease even in sleep.

Elisabetha brushed her fingers lightly once again across Vreneli's hair. She could see the storm beneath her husband's calm—the guilt, the fury, the realization that the world he thought he understood had shifted. "She's here now—safe," Elisabetha said softly.

Mathias exhaled, long and unsteady. "But Stadelmann will come looking. He'll demand she be returned."

"She will not go back."

Mathias's jaw tightened. "*Over my dead body*," he spat out.

He straightened, rubbing a hand over his face.

"I will say it again. You are not to blame for what that man has done," Elisabetha said.

"But I am responsible for what happens next."

Mathias lifted the girl gently. Together he and Elisabetha made a bed for her on the sofa in the *Stube*.

Elisabetha tucked her in. Vreneli slept restlessly, her hands curled up into fists close to her face.

Mathias turned back to his wife. "I'll speak to the authorities in Rothenburg. And to Pater Birrer. I don't like leaving the other children there even one more night."

"Yes," Elisabetha said. "But you cannot go tonight."

"No. Tonight we watch over Vreneli."

Elisabetha pulled a chair beside the sofa and sat, her hand resting on the blanket covering the girl. Mathias took the chair opposite her, the two of them forming a quiet vigil.

Upstairs, a floorboard creaked—Kandid was pacing restlessly in his room. Martina lay awake too, staring at the ceiling, listening for any sound from below. Neither child knew the truth, but both felt the rupture.

Outside, the wind moved through the fields, brushing against the shutters. The moon rose, casting pale light across the yard.

Inside, the Stirnimann home held its fragile warmth around the wounded child.

And in the quiet that followed, the truth settled into the bones of the house—a truth that could not be silenced.

Chapter Thirty-Six
Mathias's Resolve

Mathias had not slept. When the first light touched the windows, he was already dressed, pacing restlessly in the kitchen. Elisabetha rose from her chair in the *Stube* quietly, her face pale with the exhaustion of the night before.

He looked at his wife as if weighing something heavy.

"Elisabetha," he said, "if it comes to it…would you take all six children? At least for now?"

She didn't ask why. She didn't ask how. She simply nodded once.

"If they need us," she said, "we will take them."

Mathias exhaled slowly, his worry for the *Verdingkinder's* immediate future loosening its grip on him. He kissed his wife's forehead, took his coat, and stepped into the cold morning.

Der Friedensrichter first stopped at the rectory of the Marienkirche. Pater Birrer opened the door before Mathias could knock, as if he had been waiting.

"You've heard," Mathias said.

Birrer nodded grimly. "Come in."

They sat at the small wooden table in the priest's study. Mathias told him everything—the girl's arrival, the doctor's words, the other children still on the farm.

When he finished, the priest folded his hands. "God is showing you how to be of service, Mathias. Don't you see? These children were brought to your door for a reason."

"I don't know if we can manage six," Mathias said quietly.

"Not forever, perhaps," Birrer replied. "But for now. Could you take them at Ottorüthi until proper homes can be found?"

Mathias stared at the grain of the table. He already knew the answer.

"*Ja*," he said. "We can."

Pater Birrer placed a hand on his shoulder. "Then go. Do what must be done. And God be with you."

Mathias rode hard to Rothenburg. The cold air stung his face, but he didn't slow. At the *Amtsgericht*, he dismounted and strode inside, boots echoing on the stone floor.

He filed criminal charges against Kaspar Stadelmann.

He notified them of the doctor's report.

He gave his own testimony.

He described the six *Verdingkinder* on the farm—underfed, overworked, physically abused, and in danger.

He gave the name of the girl who had been assaulted: Vreneli.

The magistrate consulted the contract records and found her full name as well as the names of the other five children.

The official listened without interruption, his expression tightening as the details unfolded. When Mathias finished, the man reached for a pen.

"This warrants immediate action," he said.

He signed the arrest order and handed it to a clerk. Two constables were summoned—men Mathias knew by name.

"You'll accompany *Herr* Stirnimann," the magistrate said. "Bring this scoundrel in."

The constables nodded. Mathias thanked the judicial official, turned, and walked out with the warrant in his coat pocket.

Der Friedensrichter took the lead on horseback, the constables following in the cart that would carry Stadelmann back. They rode toward the farm in silence. The yard looked the same as it had the day before—sagging buildings, scattered tools, the air heavy with neglect.

Stadelmann stepped out of the barn when he heard the horses. His eyes narrowed when he saw the constables.

"What's this?" he demanded.

Mathias unfolded the warrant and held it before him. "Kaspar Stadelmann, you are under arrest."

"For what?" he thundered.

"*You know very well for what*," Mathias snarled—though he was not a man who snarled. "For the abuse and neglect of the children placed with you by the *Kanton* of Luzern!"

The constables moved in. Stadelmann tried to pull away, but they were stronger. They bound his wrists, fastened the chains, and marched him toward the cart.

He spat at the ground. "*Lies!* All of it! You'll regret this, Stirnimann!"

Mathias didn't answer. He watched as they lifted Stadelmann into the cart and secured him. The miserable wretch cursed the entire time, his voice cracking with rage.

The constables climbed onto the bench and one took the reins.

"We'll take him straight to the jail in Rothenburg," the other said.

Mathias nodded.

The cart lurched forward, wheels grinding over the frozen earth. Stadelmann's shouts faded as they moved down the road.

Mathias remained in the yard for a moment, the cold settling around him. The farm was silent now. Too silent.

He glanced toward the barn and then the house.

No children in sight.

They were hiding. Of course they were.

He could feel their eyes somewhere in the shadows—watching, waiting, not daring to hope.

Only after the cart disappeared did a small face appear between the slats of the barn wall, then another, and another. Thin, frightened, unsure.

Mathias didn't approach them.

Not yet.

He simply nodded once, letting them see that their master was gone.

Yet again, he looked toward the barn where the children had worked and slept. Toward the fields where they had labored from before dawn until after dark.

It was over.

But the work ahead—the real work—had only begun.

He mounted his horse and turned toward home.

The children would not be left there another night.

Not while he still drew breath.

Chapter Thirty-Seven
The Children Come Home

Mathias reached Ottorüthi before noon. The air was sharp, the sky low and gray. Uli was in the yard, splitting kindling. He looked up when his master rode in and read everything in his face without a word.

"Get two men," Mathias said. "We're going there now."

Uli nodded once and went to fetch them. Within minutes the three *Knechte* were ready. Uli took the reins of the horse cart; the other two climbed into the back with their coats buttoned tight. Their expressions were grim. No one spoke.

The only sound was the horses' hooves thudding over the frozen ground.

The Stadelmann farm looked even worse in the midday sun. The muddy yard was littered with broken tools, rotting boards, and the bloated carcasses of several dead rats. The house slumped, weary with age. The barn door hung crooked on its hinges.

No children in sight.

Mathias dismounted. "They're hiding," he said quietly. "Go easy," he cautioned his men.

Uli and the *Knechte* began searching the outbuildings. They moved slowly, not wanting to startle anyone. In the barn, the smell hit them first—ammonia, rot, unwashed bodies. The hay was black with filth. Rat droppings covered the floor.

"God help them," one of the *Knechte* murmured.

A faint rustle came from the hayloft. Uli climbed the ladder and found three boys pressed against the far wall, thin as rails, eyes wide with fear. They didn't speak. They didn't move.

"It's all right," Uli said, voice low. "Your master is gone. *Er hockt im Gefängnis.* No one will hurt you now."

The boys didn't believe him, not yet.

Outside, Mathias walked toward the woodshed. A small boy's face peered out from behind the stacked logs. He froze when he saw the giant of a man. Every muscle in him was ready to bolt. Mathias crouched down so he wasn't towering over him.

"You're safe," he said gently. "Truly safe."

The child didn't come to him freely, but he didn't run away, either.

An older girl emerged next, stepping out from behind the chicken coop. She looked older than her years, shoulders squared as if bracing for a blow.

Mathias stood and addressed them all, his voice steady.

"My name is *Herr* Stirnimann. Please tell me your names," Mathias said. "Every one of you."

They hesitated, glancing at one another. Speaking their names felt dangerous—as if names could be taken, or used against them.

The older girl stepped forward first. "I am Maria."

The small boy emerged from the shed, stepping out from behind the stacked logs. "Seppi," he whispered.

Hans-Ueli came forward next, placing himself where the younger ones could see him. "Hans-Ueli," he said, steady.

Ruedi and Kobi came after him, shoulder to shoulder.

"Ruedi."

"Kobi."

They stood in a line, silent, waiting for whatever came next.

Mathias stepped forward and shook each child's hand. His grip was firm, respectful, the way he would greet any adult.

"You will never spend another hour on this farm," he said. "Not one more. I give you my solemn vow."

The words hung in the cold air. The children stared at him, trying to understand a promise they had never heard before.

"Gather what belongs to you," Mathias said. "Anything that's yours."

They looked around helplessly. There was nothing, really. A wooden spoon. A ragged blanket. A pair of shoes with the soles worn through. Maria found a scrap of cloth she had used as a kerchief. Ruedi put a bit of twine in his pocket. Kobi had nothing at all except for the tattered clothes on his back.

The sight pierced Mathias's heart. "That's enough," Mathias said gently. "Come."

Mathias guided the children to the cart and the boys climbed in. Uli took the reins. The horses started forward.

Der Friedensrichter looked back once at the Stadelmann farm—the broken fences, the bowed roof, the yard littered with ruin—then turned away.

"Home," he said quietly, as if to himself. "We're going home."

They rode back to Ottorüthi in silence. The cart rolled down the frozen road, creaking as it carried the children, their thin bodies swaying with each jolt of the wheels. Seppi rode with Mathias, his small hands gripping the pommel of the saddle. Maria and Hans-Ueli, the two eldest, walked beside the cart for part of the way, insisting they could manage on their own feet.

Behind them lay the old life. Ahead lay the new.

Chapter Thirty-Eight
The House of Refuge

Elisabetha heard the cart before she saw it—the slow grind of wheels on frozen earth, the horses blowing steam into the cold air. She wiped her hands on her apron and stepped out into the yard.

The cart came to a halt. Mathias dismounted first, carrying Seppi in his strong arms. Then the other children jumped out of the cart.

They stood clustered together, thin and silent, their clothes hanging off them like rags pulled from a ditch. None of them looked up. They seemed unsure of what to do.

Elisabetha felt her breath catch. She had known there were five more coming—but she had not grasped what five more meant. She thought she had prepared herself, but the sight of them—their hollow cheeks, their torn, filthy clothing, their wary eyes—struck her like a blow.

Mathias met her eyes. He didn't speak. He didn't need to.

Elisabetha stepped forward. "I am *Frau* Stirnimann. Welcome to Ottorüthi. Come inside out of the cold," she said gently. "All of you."

Not one of them moved. They hesitated, as if crossing into the house might be a trap. Mathias placed a hand on Hans-Ueli's shoulder and guided him forward.

"This is your home," he said. "At least for now."

The word *home* made Maria flinch. Kobi looked up sharply, as if he had misheard.

But they stepped inside and found Vreneli waiting for them.

The others followed, not because they trusted, but because they had nowhere else to go.

Elisabetha opened the door wide. Warm air drifted out—it smelled of broth, of bread, of a house that provided comfort.

They crossed the threshold like creatures entering a world they had only heard about in *Märchen*.

The children stopped just past the door of the big farm kitchen, as if afraid to go farther. Their eyes moved over the room—the tile stove, the wooden table, the shelves lined with crockery—but they did not touch anything. They stood with their backs to the wall, ready to flee if necessary.

Elisabetha kept her voice steady. "You'll need washing first. All of you. Then clothes. Then food."

She led the two girls toward the washroom in the rear of the house, where a *Knecht* had already hauled buckets of hot water. Steam curled upward in soft clouds. The children froze at the sight of it—hot water was a luxury they had never known. A curtain had been hung across the corner where the basins waited, giving the girls a measure of privacy.

"You'll wash here," Elisabetha said softly. "There's plenty of warm water for you both."

They stared at the floor, unsure whether they were being tested.

She turned to Maria first. "Go behind the curtain," she advised kindly. "You can help Vreneli. Take your time. There are soft, clean cloths and soap."

Maria hesitated, then nodded. She guided Vreneli behind the curtain, whispering something meant to steady the little girl. Elisabetha stayed close—near enough to help if needed, far enough to give them privacy.

Behind the curtain, Vreneli whimpered. "It's all right," Maria murmured to her. "It's only warm water."

Elisabetha stepped in only when Maria called softly, "I think I need your help with her. She is afraid."

Vreneli stood trembling, arms wrapped tightly around her thin, naked body. Elisabetha knelt and washed her quickly with a soapy cloth, respectfully, speaking in low, soothing tones. The child leaned into her like a frightened animal, but she did not pull away.

When they were done, Elisabetha wrapped her in a blanket. Vreneli clung to her sleeve, exhausted.

When Maria emerged, her hair dripping, Elisabetha offered her a towel. "May I help with your hair?" she asked, comb in hand.

Maria swallowed and hesitated when she saw the lice comb. Then she sat down without a word, her shoulders sagging.

Elisabetha worked gently, careful not to pull too hard. It was no surprise. Neglected children often carried lice. She worked the comb carefully through Maria's hair, tactfully saying nothing of what she found. The girl's shoulders slowly loosened. When Elisabetha was finished, she turned her attention toward Vreneli's head of wet blonde curls.

The boys waited in the hall, stiff and anxious. Mathias stepped forward.

"Come on, *Buebe*," he said. "We'll wash in the south barn. There's a stove going."

They followed him reluctantly. Elisabetha watched them go—four thin backs, four sets of shoulders braced for blows that would not come.

In the barn, a *Knecht* had set out large basins of steaming water behind a blanket strung up for privacy. "Soap and washcloths are on the bench," Mathias said. "Water's hot. No one will bother you."

Hans-Ueli stripped down and washed first, quick and silent. Ruedi scrubbed at the layers of dirt on his body until his skin reddened. Seppi tried to hide the rat bites on his legs. Kobi shivered so hard the water sloshed over the rim of the basin.

Mathias didn't touch them. He simply stood nearby, humming under his breath, the way one might soothe a skittish horse. He noted the rat bites on their legs and arms; they would all need tending. He thought of the calendula and pine resin salves Uli kept in the cupboard for his *Knechte*—the *Ringelblumensalbe* for healing, the harsher *Harzsalbe* that drew infection out of a wound. He'd ask for a jar of each before nightfall.

When they finished, he handed each boy a blanket and nodded toward the house. "Go on. *Frau* Stirnimann has clothes for you."

The boys exchanged uncertain glances—privacy, warmth, and gentleness were all new to them—but they obeyed.

Back in the house, Elisabetha had laid out clothing on the kitchen table: underclothes, patched shirts, woolen stockings, skirts, and trousers that didn't match but were clean and whole.

Maria touched the hem of her new skirt. "I've never had something without holes," she whispered.

"You do now," Elisabetha said.

The boys dressed awkwardly, unused to garments that fit. Kobi kept smoothing the long, cuffed sleeves of his shirt, as if afraid it might vanish.

When they were all clothed and wrapped in blankets, they looked less like shadows and more like children—wary, exhausted, but human again.

By early evening, the table was set. It had been many years since the old farmhouse table at Ottorüthi had held so many. The children sat stiffly, hands in their laps, afraid to touch anything.

Mathias took his seat at the head. He and his family bowed their heads as he said the blessing over the meal. The six *Verdingkinder* sat frozen, unsure of the rules in this new house.

Mathias lifted his head and nodded toward the bowls. "Eat," he said gently. "That's all you need to do." They still didn't move.

Elisabetha realized they were waiting for permission—or punishment.

She picked up her spoon and took a bite of pork stew. "See?"

Hans-Ueli reached for his spoon first, his hand shaking. Then Maria. Then the others. They ate quickly at first, as if afraid the food might vanish, then slowed down to savor it.

At one point, Kobi dropped his spoon. He flinched violently, shrinking from the slap he thought was coming. Mathias bent down, picked up the spoon, wiped it on his linen napkin, and set it back in front of the boy.

"No harm done," he said with a smile.

Kobi stared at him, open-mouthed.

After supper, the sleeping arrangements were explained.

"Kandid will take Seppi," Mathias said. "There's enough room for two in his chamber."

Seppi looked startled, as if he had been offered a place in a palace.

"Vreneli will sleep with Martina," Elisabetha said. "Maria, you'll have the sofa in the *Stube*. It can be made quite cozy with sheets, blankets, and a pillow."

Maria nodded, though she looked as if she didn't quite believe it.

"The other three boys," Mathias continued, "will sleep in the hayloft. Fresh sheets and blankets until we can get proper cots."

He grinned at the boys. "It's warm up there. And no rats."

Ruedi's eyes widened. "None at all?"

Mathias winked. "Not a one. I'd stake my life on it."

The boys exchanged glances—the first flicker of hope.

That night, Elisabetha helped Vreneli into her daughter's bed. The child lay stiffly, her eyes wide in the dim light.

"You're safe," Elisabetha said.

Vreneli didn't answer. She simply reached out and gripped Elisabetha's sleeve, holding on until sleep finally claimed her.

"Isn't she beautiful, Mama?" Martina whispered, as they both gazed at the sleeping child. Elisabetha smiled.

In the *Stube*, Maria lay awake on the sofa, staring at the ceiling. When Elisabetha passed through to bank the stove, Maria whispered, "Do we have to leave tomorrow?"

"*Nai*," Elisabetha said. "You'll stay here for now. No one will send you away in the morning."

Maria nodded, but her eyes filled with tears she refused to let fall.

In the barn, the boys settled into the hayloft. Uli had laid out blankets and sheets on the mounds of fresh hay. Once they had settled under the covers, he tucked warm bricks at their feet. Hans-Ueli lay on his back, staring at the rafters.

"Is this real?" Kobi whispered.

Hans-Ueli said nothing. The lump in his throat made speech impossible.

When the house finally quieted, Mathias and Elisabetha sat together at the kitchen table. The lamp flickered between them.

"It will be hard," Elisabetha said to her husband.

"*Ja.* But let's not forget these aren't helpless children. They can do much for themselves."

"Six children. And our two besides."

"Yes."

She folded her hands. "But they're here now."

Mathias nodded.

Outside, the wind rattled the shutters. Inside, the house held a new, fragile warmth—the warmth of a refuge just beginning to take shape.

Chapter Thirty-Nine
Learning to Live

The next days and months passed in their own rough order. Finally, life settled into a rhythm, though no one would have called it easy. The children woke early, blinking at the unfamiliar warmth of real blankets, the smell of bread baking in the kitchen, the sound of Mathias moving through the yard.

They watched everything. They trusted nothing yet.

Mathias entrusted the boys to his *Knechte.* He knew that the kind, fatherly Uli would make the work an invitation. Nothing heavy. Nothing that would break their backs or their spirits.

"Will you carry this into the barn for me, *Bueb*?" he asked Hans-Ueli, handing him a sack of oats. "Not more."

Hans-Ueli nodded, surprised by the weight—or rather, by the lack of it. At Stadelmann's, he had hauled sacks four times as heavy, and the beatings had come when he faltered. Now he carried the oats across the yard with a lightness he hadn't felt in years.

Ruedi and Kobi swept the stable aisles. They worked diligently, glancing at the *Knechte* every now and then. Uli corrected their grip on the broom, nothing more.

"You'll get it," he said with a smile. "Everything takes its own time."

The boys stared at him, unsure how to answer such kindness.

Inside, Elisabetha gathered the girls.

"Just small things," she said. "Folding linens. Shelling beans. Nothing more."

Maria nodded, eager to do well. Vreneli clung to her side, eyes darting around the kitchen as if danger might spring from the cupboards.

Elisabetha set a basket of clean napkins on the table. "We fold these in half. Then in half again."

Maria's fingers moved carefully, reverently. She had never handled anything so fine. Vreneli copied her, though her folds were crooked. When she dropped one, she froze, breath held tight.

"It's all right, *Chind*," Elisabetha said with a smile. "Just pick it up." Vreneli did, but she trembled all the while.

❦

Every afternoon, when the sun slipped behind the ridge, Elisabetha gathered all six children and walked with them across the yard to the barn library. The boys were excused from chores at that hour; even the *Knechte* stepped aside as they passed, as if recognizing the solemnity of what was about to happen. The children moved in a tight cluster, unsure whether this new privilege could be trusted.

The barn library smelled of book pages and old wood. The narrow iron stove the *Knechte* had installed long ago glowed faintly in one corner. The light from the high window fell in long, fading stripes across the floorboards. The children stopped just inside the doorway, as if afraid to enter. "This is where we'll learn," Elisabetha said.

No one moved.

They sat on benches with slate boards in their laps. Elisabetha placed a piece of chalk in each hand. Maria held hers delicately, as though it might break. Seppi pinched his between two fingers. Ruedi gripped his too tightly. Hans-Ueli held his like a nail, ready to hammer it.

"Like this," Elisabetha said, guiding Maria's fingers.

"Not so tight," Martina murmured to Ruedi.

"Let it rest," she told Seppi.

She gently adjusted Hans-Ueli's grip. He stared at his own hand as if it belonged to someone else.

None of them made a mark.

Elisabetha drew a large A on her slate, the chalk making a soft, steady line.

"This is where we begin. This sound," she said, touching the letter with her fingertip. "*Ah.*"

The children watched her mouth, not the slate.

"*Ah,*" she repeated, slower this time.

Maria whispered it back.

Seppi mouthed it without sound.

Ruedi stared at the letter as if it were a strange tool he'd never seen.

Hans-Ueli didn't speak at all, but his eyes followed the movement of her lips.

"Now you try on your slate," Elisabetha instructed.

They tried—halting, uneven, shy—but they tried.

Vreneli drew a squiggle with her chalk. Maria made a trembling line. Seppi made a dot. Ruedi pressed too hard and snapped his chalk. Kobi wiped his slate clean before anyone could see his crooked attempt. Hans-Ueli froze entirely, his face tightening with shame. He was afraid to make a mistake, for surely a cuff on the ear would follow it.

Martina knelt beside him. "It's only a line," she whispered. "Nothing more."

He swallowed and tentatively copied the lines that formed the letter.

The older children struggled the most. Illiteracy was not just a lack of skill—it was a wound. Hans-Ueli's face burned when his lines wavered. Ruedi hid his slate behind his arm. Kobi erased every mark before anyone could praise or correct him. Even Maria, eager as she was, flinched each time her chalk squeaked.

Elisabetha never raised her voice. Neither she nor her daughter ever uttered a harsh word.

"You're learning," they said brightly.

"Let's try again," Martina suggested.

But after a few more attempts, the children's shoulders sagged.

Elisabetha stepped in. "That's enough for today."

After each lesson, she let them wander the shelves. They couldn't read a word, but they touched the spines, traced the gold lettering, lifted covers as if opening treasure chests. Maria held a book to her chest. Seppi smelled the pages. Hans-Ueli stared at an engraving of a mountain and whispered, "Is that real?" The barn library became a place of wonder for them.

Weeks passed before anything changed. One afternoon, Maria wrote a perfect A—not shaky, not crooked. A real letter. Elisabetha smiled. "*Schön.*" Maria's eyes filled, and she wiped them quickly, embarrassed. Ruedi managed a straight line. Seppi wrote a crooked *I* that looked like a snake. Hans-Ueli formed the first letter of his name—a tentative, uneven H—and stared at it as if it had appeared by magic.

They were still illiterate. But they had taken their first steps into the world of letters.

Day after day, the lessons continued: chalk dust on their fingers, the scrape of slates, Elisabetha's calm voice, Martina's gentle corrections, the smell of old books and ink, the slow, steady forming of letters. The boys stopped dreading the hour. The girls even began to look forward to it. The barn library was the place where something new was taking shape—not quickly, not easily, but with a steadiness that felt like hope.

Trust came slowly to the children, in moments so small they might have been missed.

Kobi hummed under his breath while sweeping.

Ruedi laughed once—a short, startled bleat—when a barn cat leapt onto Hans-Ueli's lap and nearly sent his slate flying.

Seppi leaned against Mathias's body without realizing it.

But the nights were harder.

Vreneli woke screaming, her voice raw, her small body thrashing. She bit anyone who tried to hold her. Martina sat beside her, helpless, whispering her name.

Elisabetha carried the little girl into the kitchen, where the lamp still burned low. She reached for the book of Bible parables that now resided on the kitchen shelf. It opened naturally to the story of the Prodigal Son, its pages worn soft from years of handling.

"*Look*," she murmured. "See the boy coming home?"

Vreneli stared at the picture, breath hitching. Her fingers touched the painted figure, tracing the father's outstretched arms. Slowly, her sobs quieted. Leaning against Elisabetha's shoulder, she drifted into an exhausted sleep.

Mathias waited until the ground had dried enough to give under their feet. He led the boys to the meadow behind the north barn, the grass still bent from winter but softening in the sun. A faint dampness still clung to the earth, the last of winter working its way out of the ground.

"*Schwingen* first," he said, as if the word needed no explanation. "We Swiss wrestle not to hurt others, but to learn strength without anger, and balance—of the body and of the temper."

He showed them how to plant their feet, how to grip a shoulder, how to fall without fear. The boys watched him with the wary attention of animals who had learned to expect pain.

"Try," he said.

Ruedi stepped forward first—not because he was eager, but because he knew the younger ones would follow his lead. Mathias paired him with Hans-Ueli. They circled each other, awkward at first, then with a growing sense of play. When Hans-Ueli slipped and Ruedi toppled over him, both boys froze, waiting for the reprimand.

Mathias only laughed. "Good. Again."

The tension broke.

Ruedi grinned.

Hans-Ueli tried a new grip.

Ruedi planted his feet more firmly, surprised by the strength in his own body.

They wrestled until their shirts clung to their backs. Mathias watched them settle, gauging their strength, their eagerness. Then he picked up a smooth stone from the edge of the field.

"*Steinstossen*," he said. "A good skill. Teaches more than strength. Timing. Control. Knowing when to hold and when to release."

He held the stone at his neck, elbow high, and sent it arcing across the meadow. The boys watched it land with a soft thud.

"One at a time."

Seppi went first. His throw was short, but clean.

Kobi's stone slipped from his hand and rolled a few feet; he laughed, embarrassed.

Ruedi's stone flew in a crooked line but farther than he expected.

Hans-Ueli surprised them all—his stone sailed nearly as far as Mathias's.

Mathias nodded. "You've got good shoulders."

Hans-Ueli looked down, hiding the small, startled pride that rose inside himself.

They kept at it until their arms trembled. The meadow filled with the sound of stones landing in the grass—soft, steady, hopeful.

In the late afternoons, when the lessons were completed and the light slanted low across the yard, the house filled with the soft clatter of work. Elisabetha peeled potatoes at the kitchen table. Maria shelled peas beside her. Seppi swept the floor in slow, careful strokes. Even Vreneli, when she wasn't clinging to Maria's skirt, stacked kindling in a small basket.

Elisabetha began to sing without thinking—a folksong she had learned from her own mother.

Lueget, vo Bärgen und Tal
Flieht scho der Sunnestrahl!
Lueget, uf Auen und Matte
Wachse die dunkele Schatte;
D Sunn uf de Bärge no stoht.
O, wie si d Gletscher so rot!

The words were simple, the melody older than memory.

Maria looked up, startled. She had never heard an adult sing while working. At Stadelmann's, sound had meant danger—boots, shouts, blows. But this was different. This was a woman singing because her hands were busy and her heart was untroubled.

Seppi paused in his sweeping, listening.

Kobi drifted in from the yard, drawn by the sound.

Ruedi stood in the doorway, arms crossed, unsure what to do with the warmth that rose inside him.

Elisabetha kept peeling, her voice soft but sure.

Martina joined her from the hearth, adding her sweet soprano to the second verse.

Lueget, do aben a See!

Heimetzuet wendet si 's Veh;

Loset, wie d Glogge, die schöne,

Fründlig im Moos 's ertöne.

Chüejerglüt, üseri Lust,

Tuet 's so wohl i der Brust!

The refrain rose and fell like breath.

Maria began to hum along, barely audible.

Kobi tried the tune under his breath, missing half the notes.

Seppi tapped the broom handle against his leg in time.

Even Ruedi's shoulders loosened, though he didn't sing.

As she continued preparations for the evening meal, Elisabetha shifted into a lighter song, playful and rhythmic.

Wen-i nume wüsst,

wo 's Vogel-Lisi wär.

'S Vogel-Lisi chunnt vo Adelbode här.

Adelbode isch im Bärner Oberland.

'S Bärner Oberland isch schö-ö-ön.

'S Oberland, ja 's Oberland,

's Bärner Oberland isch schön.

'S Oberland, ja 's Oberland,

's Bärner Oberland isch schön.

The words alone were enough to make Seppi grin.

Maria laughed softly.

Kobi echoed the refrain, shy but eager.

Vreneli swayed where she stood, her small hands opening and closing in time with the melody.

Ruedi stayed silent, but his eyes softened. He watched the others, watched the way the room changed when voices filled it. The kitchen felt warmer, not from the stove but from the sound itself—a warmth he had never known.

The songs threaded through the work, binding the children to the farm's daily rhythms. They didn't know the lyrics yet, but they learned the shape of the song—its rise and fall, the way a melody could carry a task forward. They learned that singing was joyful. They learned that sound could be safe.

When the last notes faded, the room held a quiet that felt different from silence—not fear, not waiting, but rest.

Elisabetha had learned that music could be healing. She noticed it first with Vreneli. One afternoon she had worked herself into a trembling state, her small body tight as a fist, her breath coming in sharp, frightened bursts. Elisabetha lifted her gently and carried her to the rocking chair by the stove. The others kept working, quieter now, watching from the corners of their eyes.

Elisabetha began to sing—a lullaby not only meant for sleep, but the kind a mother sings when a child has been overstimulated. It settled over Vreneli like a hand smoothing a rumpled cloth.

Schlaf, Chindli, schlaf,
der Vater hütet d'Schaf.
Die Mueter schüttlet 's Bäumeli,
da falle viili Träumeli.
Schlaf, Chindli, schlaf.

The melody was simple, steady, gentle. Vreneli stiffened at first. Then her hands loosened. Her head dropped against Elisabetha's shoulder. The rocking slowed. The singing continued, soft and unbroken. Maria wiped her eyes with the back of her hand. Seppi swept more quietly. Even Ruedi paused in the doorway, listening. When the last notes faded, Vreneli was asleep, her breath warm against Elisabetha's neck. The room held its breath with her.

After some months, singing had become part of the household. Not every day, but often enough that the children no longer froze when Elisabetha began a tune. Maria sang freely. Kobi hummed. Seppi tried to match the rhythm with whatever tool he held. Ruedi never sang. He listened from a slight distance, arms crossed or hands in his pockets, watching the others with a look that was half longing, half disbelief.

One evening, as they peeled carrots at the table, Elisabetha began to sing a familiar folksong.

Da höch uf de Alpe, dem Hüttli nid färn, da hüet i mini Geissli, da bin i so gern.

Tralalala…

Da lacht mer de Himmel höch über em Schnee und Matte voll Blüemli, so schön 's will gsee.

Tralalala…

Martina joined her. Maria followed. Seppi's voice wavered in and out. Ruedi kept his eyes on the carrots. His jaw tightened. Then, almost too quietly to hear, he shaped a single line of the melody. Not the whole song—just a fragment, barely voiced. Maria looked up, startled. Kobi grinned. Elisabetha didn't turn her head or pause her work. She simply kept singing, as if nothing unusual had happened. Ruedi's voice faded as quickly as it had come, but the sound of it—that one thin, uncertain line—stayed in the room long after.

The following month, Mathias was stacking wood in the yard, the steady thud of logs filling the silence. He paused to wipe his brow but then heard another sound threading faintly through the open kitchen window. Voices. Not crying. Not shouting. Not the tense silence he had grown used to. Singing. His wife's voice first—low, sure. His daughter's sweet harmony. Maria's clear, small thread. Seppi's uneven hum. Kobi's off-key enthusiasm. And beneath it all, a deeper note—hesitant, almost hidden. Since Hans-Ueli was working with the *Knechte* most days now, it had to be Ruedi, he thought.

Mathias stood still, one hand on the woodpile. The sound drifted across the yard, thin but steady, like smoke rising from a chimney. Something shifted inside him—not relief, not triumph, but a quiet recognition. He set the last log in place and listened until the song ended. Then he went inside.

A fragile new life was taking shape at Ottorüthi, one song at a time. The children were changing. Something beautiful was beginning to take root—not healing, not yet, but the shape of it.

At night, when the young ones slept, Mathias and Elisabetha spoke in low tones in their bedroom.

"They're learning," Elisabetha whispered.

"Yes," Mathias said. "And perhaps something more." His wife smiled at him.

Outside, the wind moved through the trees. Inside, the house held its new warmth—growing, day by day, into something stronger that might last.

Chapter Forty
The Hearing

The legal proceeding against Kaspar Stadelmann was held behind closed doors in a small chamber within the magistrate's office in Rothenburg. No public gallery, no crowd. Just a table, several chairs, and the magistrate's *Protokollbuch* open before him. The shutters were half-closed against the afternoon light, leaving the room dim and cool.

Mathias and Elisabetha entered with Vreneli and Maria. The magistrate nodded once, his expression unreadable, and motioned for them to sit. His quill rested beside the open book, ink still wet from the last case.

He began with Vreneli.

Elisabetha lifted the child onto her lap. Vreneli clung to her, small hands gripping the fabric of her dress. The magistrate spoke gently, his voice low enough not to startle her. The jolly man with the twinkling eyes did not speak of the case at first; he told her instead about his grandson, whom he said looked to be about her age. Only after a few such harmless remarks did his tone grow serious.

"Tell me why you went with *Herr* Stadelmann into the woods," he said.

Vreneli pressed her face into Elisabetha's shoulder. Her voice came out thin, almost a whisper.

"He said…he said he had a doll for me. A real one. With golden hair and blue eyes. A china doll." She swallowed. "He said she was hiding in the forest and I had to come with him to find her. Then she would be my baby forever."

Elisabetha's arms tightened around her.

The magistrate had to swallow hard before he could speak. "And when you went there with him," he asked, "what happened?"

Vreneli shook her head once, as if trying to dislodge the memory. "He made me lie down," she whispered. "On the moss. He said I had to be very quiet. He said it was a game." Her small hands twisted in Elisabetha's sleeve. "I didn't want to," she whispered. "But he held me down and hurt me inside my body. I don't know exactly what he did or why it hurt so much."

She could not say more. She didn't need to.

The magistrate nodded slowly, his face grave. "You have told me enough," he said. "You have done a very brave thing today, Vreneli. Thank you, *Chind*."

She slid down from Elisabetha's lap and let herself be led outside where Martina and the boys would watch her while Maria gave her testimony.

The teenager sat stiffly in the chair, eyes downcast, hands folded in her lap. She kept her eyes glued to the magistrate's desk, not on his face. Her voice was steadier than Vreneli's, but the tremor beneath it was unmistakable.

"I saw him take her," she said. "I saw him lead her into the trees. I knew what he would do. He had done it to me before…many times." Her voice wavered but did not break. "He told me not to speak, or he would kill us all. He said no one would believe a *Verdingchind*, anyway."

The magistrate's jaw tightened.

Maria continued, her words coming in short, controlled bursts. "He would take me behind the barn. Or into the shed. He said it was my fault. That I tempted him. But later, Hans-Ueli helped me. To escape him." She began to sob quietly. "That's when he went after Vreneli. I tried to stop him. I tried. But he hit me. I couldn't help her. It is my fault."

She covered her face with her hands. Elisabetha and Mathias each laid a hand on her shoulders, anchoring her.

"You are a child, Maria," the magistrate said, his tone low but firm. "You are not responsible for this man's crimes."

Maria nodded once, though she did not look up.

The magistrate then interviewed the boys. He wrote for a long time after taking down all of their testimony, including that of the Stirnimanns. The scratch of the quill was the only sound in the room. When he finally set it aside, he folded his hands and spoke with the solemnity of a man who understood the weight of his words.

"Kaspar Stadelmann is found guilty on all counts," he said. "He will serve life imprisonment. His farm and property are hereby seized by the *Kanton* of Luzern. The livestock will remain with Mathias Stirnimann. The land and buildings will be auctioned."

The magistrate closed the *Protokollbuch* with a soft thud.

"You are free to leave," he said. "I will read the verdict to the defendant separately." He paused for a few moments, his voice lower when he spoke again. "And may God bless each of you."

Outside, the air was cold and bright. The children blinked against the light as if emerging from a pitch dark room. Mathias placed a hand on Ruedi's shoulder. Hans-Ueli walked with Maria. Elisabetha carried Vreneli, who had fallen asleep against her neck. Martina held hands with Kobi and Seppi.

They walked back toward the wagon in silence where Kandid was waiting in the driver's seat—it was not the tense silence of fear, but the solemn quiet that follows truth spoken aloud.

Something terrible had ended. The harm would live in them for years, perhaps for the rest of their lives.

But the man who caused it could not touch them again.

In that small mercy, healing began.

Chapter Forty-One
Years of Harvest

The years that followed did not hurry. They came the way seasons do on a farm—quietly, steadily, without asking permission. The land kept its rhythm. The children grew into their bodies, their voices, their work. What had been broken did not vanish, but it no longer ruled their days.

Mathias sometimes stood in the doorway at dusk and watched his adopted children—six young lives moving through chores with the ease of belonging. He had once imagined a large family, but he had never pictured this: a table crowded with elbows and laughter, boots lined in pairs by the door, the sight of many hands working in the fields. He and Elisabetha did not speak of it often, but both felt it. These were *their* children now, every one of them. They could not imagine their lives without them.

The barn library became the quiet center of daily life. The floor was now covered with braided rag rugs. The wooden shelves built by Mathias's *Knechte* years ago still held the many volumes Elisabetha had brought with her from Sins at the time of her second marriage, including many more since then. The books stood in neat rows, their spines worn, their pages softened by many hands.

She had taught the children to read and write there. At first, it was slow work. Ruedi stumbled over letters, jaw clenched with effort. Seppi copied words into a small notebook he kept in his pocket. Kobi learned numbers through farm accounts, tracing sums with a blunt pencil. Maria read aloud to the younger ones, her voice steady and patient. Vreneli traced letters with her finger on the table, whispering their sounds under her breath. The library Elisabetha had built shaped them all.

She never hurried them. She sat with each child in turn, her voice low, her instruction gentle. She also taught them to care for books as if they were living things—never to crease a page, never to leave one open on its face, always to return it to its proper place. In time, the library became more than a room. It became a place where the children learned not only to read, but to think, to imagine, to belong.

The eldest two were the first to step into their own futures. Hans-Ueli grew tall and steady, a young man who carried responsibility without complaint.

Maria, quiet but sure-handed, learned to manage a household with a competence that surprised even her.

Their wedding was small, held in the Marienkirche in Bertiswil with only family and a few kind neighbors in attendance. Elisabetha dressed Maria's hair before the ceremony, a quiet act that needed no words. Afterward, Mathias and Kandid helped Hans-Ueli to load the wagon for their move to Aargau. The young couple would go to the Villiger farm outside Geltwil to help care for Elisabetha's aging parents, staying on as paid servants. Maria wrote letters home—her careful, neat script learned in the barn loft a testament to her adopted mother's patient teaching. Elisabetha kept each one folded carefully in a drawer, tucked among sprigs of lavender.

Ruedi grew into his strength slowly, like a tree taking root. He was welcomed by Mathias and Kandid as a trusted *Knecht* at Ottorüthi, rising before dawn to tend the cows and learning the craft of cheesemaking from the old dairyman who spoke little but watched everything. He kept a small notebook—temperatures, timings, the feel of curds under his hands. He wrote in it with a seriousness that would have astonished the boy he once was.

Seppi found his place in the scent of sawdust and the clean lines of wood. A carpenter in Bertiswil took him on as an apprentice, saying the boy had steady hands and a good eye. Seppi worked with a quiet intensity, shaping joints that fit cleanly, carving edges smooth as river stones. He read carpentry manuals in the barn loft, running his fingers along the diagrams as if memorizing them through touch.

Kobi grew into the land itself. He had a way with animals, a patience that calmed even the most stubborn calf. By the time he was a young man, he was managing fields of his own, walking the boundaries at dawn with a sense of purpose that made Mathias smile. He kept accounts with a precision learned in Elisabetha's library, the numbers marching neatly across the page.

Vreneli stayed close to Elisabetha, becoming her and Martina's companion in the work of the household. Elisabetha taught her to knead dough, to mend linen, to keep accounts, to manage the endless tasks that made a farm run. Vreneli learned quickly, her hands sure, her movements quiet and deliberate. Sometimes she read aloud to young visitors, the words flowing with a grace that once seemed impossible.

There were still shadows in her, moments when she startled at a sudden noise or trembled without warning. But her laughter returned in small, unforced bursts—at the barn cats' antics, at Kobi's teasing, at

Seppi's carved gifts. Elisabetha watched her with a tenderness that needed no words.

Winters came and went. Calves were born. Fields were plowed. The children's voices deepened or softened. The house changed shape around them, as houses do when the people inside them grow.

The library continued to grow, too. More books arrived—some bought, some traded, some given by neighbors and even strangers who had heard of the library of Bertiswil. The children still entered the library on quiet evenings, still opened books with reverence.

When Martina married the young veterinarian Xaver Scherer and moved to the farm her father had purchased for them, the Ölberg, the house felt her absence like a missing heartbeat. Vreneli helped her pack her linens, folding each piece with care. Elisabetha tied Martina's apron strings one last time, her fingers lingering for a moment. Mathias watched her walk down the path with her new husband, knowing she would not return to live under his roof ever again. He felt pride and loss in equal measure.

Kandid grew into his role with a quiet steadiness. When the time came, Mathias handed him the keys to Ottorüthi. The gesture was simple, but it carried the weight of a lifetime. Kandid accepted them with a nod, his face solemn. Elisabetha watched from the doorway, her eyes bright with pride. The farm had passed to the next generation.

She tried to remember the last time her first husband, Josef Moser, had crossed her mind. It had been years, she realized. The fear and the secret vow had thinned without her noticing.

Mathias walked more slowly up the hill now. The infirmities brought on by the passage of time had forced him to give up his post as *Friedensrichter* some years earlier. Elisabetha sat more often while she worked, her hands still deft but not as quick as before.

The children who remained at home took over tasks without being asked. The house was not empty, only changed in its rhythm. It was a gentler music, one shaped by years of labor and love.

On summer evenings, when the work was done, Mathias and Elisabetha sat on the bench outside the house and watched the fields darken. All eight of their children—now grown, scattered, rooted—moved through the world with purpose. The years had been long, and not easy, but they had been good.

Harvest years, every one of them.

Chapter Forty-Two
The Keeper

Vreneli and Kobi married in the parish church on a mild spring morning, the kind of day when the air smelled of thawed earth and new beginnings. They stood before the altar with hands clasped, their faces solemn and full of hope. Elisabetha watched them with a tenderness that ached. She had raised them both, though not from infancy, and now they were stepping into a life she could not follow.

Before the wedding, they came to her and Mathias with their decision. They would emigrate to America. The stigma of being *Verdingkinder* clung to them still, even as adults. It followed them into every village, every workplace, every conversation. They wanted a fresh start in a place where no one knew their past, where they could build a life without shame.

Elisabetha and Mathias listened without interrupting. They would miss their two youngest children terribly, but they understood. They had lived long enough to know that some wounds could not heal in the place where they were made.

On the morning of their departure, the wagon stood ready in the yard, loaded with the trunks, bedding, and belongings they would take across the ocean to America. Martina had come down from the Ölberg to see them off, her eyes bright with unshed tears. Mathias embraced both his children for a long time. The other members of the family embraced them one by one.

When the farewells were nearly done, Elisabetha stepped forward with a small wrapped parcel. She placed it into Vreneli's hands. When she tore off the paper, she found the picture book of Bible parables—the one with the story of the Prodigal Son, the one that had comforted her through the darkest years of her childhood. The pages were worn soft, the colors faded, the binding loose from use.

"It is yours now," Elisabetha said. "Take it with you. Let it remind you that you are loved."

Vreneli lowered her eyes, her fingers tracing the worn edge of the binding. She understood—not only the gift, but the truth behind it, the one she had first glimpsed years ago in the picture of the father running to embrace his child. She had found that kind of love in her parents, Elisabetha and Mathias.

She pressed the book to her chest, then leaned into her mother's embrace. For a moment she was the small girl who had once whispered letters under her breath in the barn library, tracing words with her finger.

Kandid would drive them only as far as Luzern, where they would take the train to Basel and then to Hamburg for the ship to New York. He would help with their trunks and see them off before turning the horses back toward Ottorüthi. She climbed onto the wagon seat beside her husband and brother. As the horses started forward, Vreneli turned and lifted her hand in a final farewell.

The wagon rolled down the road and around the bend, and then they were gone.

Three years passed before a letter came.

There was no mail delivery to Ottorüthi. Kandid brought it from the *Postamt* in Bertiswil, handing it to his mother with a smile. The envelope was battered, its edges softened, its surface stamped and restamped by postmasters across lands and oceans. Elisabetha recognized the handwriting at once. Her breath caught.

She carried the letter outside to the bench where she and Mathias had sat through so many seasons. The late afternoon light lay warm across the fields. She opened the envelope with careful fingers.

The letter told a long story.

Wisconsin had been harsh. The winters were bitter, the work unrelenting. In time, the old shame found them again. Eventually, the other Swiss immigrants learned they had been *Verdingkinder*. The whispers began. The coldness. The distance. The same old wound, carried across an ocean.

So they left.

They traveled westward, following rumors of land and opportunity. When they reached Colorado, the mountains rose around them like familiar guardians. The air was thin and bright. The earth was fertile. Through the Homestead Act, they claimed a one-hundred-sixty-acre parcel of land as their own. Kobi planted potatoes, and they flourished. They built a small house and lived far from any neighbors, but they were content. No one asked about their past. No one cared.

They were free.

Elisabetha read the letter slowly, then again. The words blurred, not due to her age, but from the weight of what they carried. She folded the pages into her lap and looked out over the fields of Ottorüthi, golden in the lowering sun.

She thought of the young woman she had been—the *stille, bescheidene Frau* who had believed her life would be small, who had believed her quietness was a kind of weakness. She thought of the vow she had made to Mathias, the vow to help him do God's work to the fullest of her ability. She had kept that vow. She saw it now with a clarity that felt like revelation.

She had tended the lives entrusted to her. She had kept her promises. She had been a keeper of secrets, a keeper of truth, a keeper of stories that needed to be witnessed. She had chosen to help even when it cost her comfort. Her actions had rippled outward into a future she would never live to see.

Her quietness had never been smallness. It had been strength. It was a part of her. It had shaped her entire life.

The librarian of Bertiswil pressed the letter to her heart, a keeper of people and promises, as surely as she had ever been a keeper of books.

Historical Afterword

This novel takes place in a world shaped by forces that governed the lives of countless real people in Switzerland throughout the nineteenth and twentieth centuries. Two of those forces—the Catholic Church's treatment of homosexuality and suicide, and the *Verdingkinder* system—left deep marks on individuals, families, and entire communities. Their histories deserve to be remembered and understood.

Homosexuality and the Catholic Church

In the nineteenth century in which this novel is set, same-sex desire was widely condemned, criminalized, and forced into silence. There was no public vocabulary for it, no safe community, and no socially acceptable way to live openly. Many men and women entered marriages they hoped would conceal or "correct" what they could not safely name, often with heartbreaking consequences for everyone involved.

The Catholic Church of that era not only regarded suicide as a mortal sin, but it also denied burial rites and barred those who died by their own hand from being laid to rest in the consecrated ground of a Catholic cemetery. This practice continued well into the twentieth century. Families were left to grieve without the comfort of ritual, and the shame surrounding such deaths often lingered for generations. These attitudes do not reflect the values of our present age, but they shaped the emotional and spiritual landscape of the time in which this story unfolds.

Verdingkinder

For generations in Switzerland, children from poor families, unmarried mothers, or households deemed "morally unfit" were taken from their homes and placed as indentured laborers on farms or in domestic service. Although the term *Verdingkinder* became common in the nineteenth century, the practice itself had earlier roots. By the 1830s, it was already an entrenched part of rural life.

These children were expected to work long hours, often with little affection or protection. Many were denied education and treated as a source of cheap labor. Survivor testimonies and historical investigations have revealed that a great number endured harsh physical punishment, chronic hunger, emotional neglect, and, in many cases, sexual abuse. Isolated and dependent on the adults who controlled their lives, they had few avenues for safety or justice.

The system persisted in various forms well into the twentieth century. Child labor placements in Switzerland continued into the 1960s. The broader coercive welfare measures that enabled such removals were not abolished until 1981. Public acknowledgment of this history—and formal apologies—came only in recent years, as survivors began to speak openly about their experiences.

A Note to the Reader

The events depicted in this novel reflect the historical realities of the nineteenth century, not the beliefs of the author. My intention is to honor the lives of those who lived under these constraints—the closeted, the shamed, the silenced, the mistreated, the displaced—and to bring to light the experiences of those who were too often abused, hidden, or ignored.

If this story has illuminated even a small part of that history, then it has served its purpose.

Glossary

This glossary provides a comprehensive alphabetical listing of the undefined words, phrases, idioms, contextual terms, and sentences in Swiss German and High German that appear in the novel. I have included approximate phonetic pronunciation notes for readers with no knowledge of these languages—though these renderings are necessarily imprecise. Song lyrics with English translations appear after the glossary.

Umlaut sounds in Swiss German are particularly difficult to convey in English, and many do not resemble their counterparts in Standard High German (for example, *ää* sounds approximately like the /a/ in the English word "bad"). Please also note that Swiss German (*Schwyzerdütsch*) has no standardized spelling system. It is a collection of regional dialects, each with its own conventions, so the same word may appear in different forms depending on the speaker's canton or village.

A

Altärli

Pronunciation: ahl-TÄÄR-lee

Meaning: "Little altar"—a diminutive form often used for a small Catholic devotional shrine in a home

alti Jungfer

Pronunciation: AHL-tee YOONG-fer

Meaning: "Old maid"; an unmarried older woman; historically carried negative social judgment

Amtsbuch (AHMTS-bookh)

Meaning: The official working book of a local magistrate or *Friedensrichter*; used to record notes, case summaries, small verdicts, fines, and observations; less formal than a court record; carried by the magistrate and written in his own hand

Amtsgericht

Pronunciation: AHMTS-geh-REEKHT

Meaning: District court; local judicial authority

B

Bauer

Pronunciation: BAU-air

Meaning: Farmer

Bauernfrau

Pronunciation: BAU-airn-frow

Meaning: Farmer's wife; a woman working on a farm

Bauernhaus

Pronunciation: BAU-airn-hows

Meaning: Farmhouse

Bauernleute

Pronunciation: BAU-airn-LOY-teh

Meaning: Farming folk; rural people

Benzenschwil

Pronunciation: BEN-tsen-shveel

Meaning: A small village in the canton of Aargau, located in the municipality of Merenschwand; historically it was a rural farming settlement along the Reuss River valley

Bertiswil

Pronunciation: BAIR-teess-veel

Meaning: A rural hamlet in the Swiss canton of Luzern

bescheiden

Pronunciation: bch-SHY-den

Meaning: Modest, humble

Biedermeier

Pronunciation: BEE-dair-my-air

Meaning: Early 19th-century Central European style; Biedermeier furniture is defined by restraint, clarity, and craftsmanship; emerged in the German-speaking world after the Napoleonic Wars, when the middle class began furnishing homes with beauty that was practical rather than aristocratic

Birrewegge

Pronunciation: BEER-reh-VECK-keh

Meaning: Literally "pear roll" or "pear log"; a traditional Swiss pastry made from a thin layer of dough rolled around a dense, sweet filling of dried pears that have been soaked, cooked down, and mixed with nuts (often walnuts), raisins, and spices. The roll is baked until the crust is golden and the filling is dark, fragrant, and almost fudge-like.

Birrewegge is especially associated with central Switzerland (Aargau, Luzern, Zug, Schwyz), where dried pears were a winter staple. It was historically a farmhouse treat—practical, nourishing, and celebratory—often baked in autumn when the pear harvest was dried for storage.

Bueb

Pronunciation: BOO-ep

Meaning: Boy (Swiss German)

Buebe

Pronunciation: BOO-ep-eh

Meaning: Boys (plural)

Büebli

Pronunciation: BEE-ep-lee

Meaning: Little boy; affectionate diminutive

C

Chääsbissen Turm

Pronunciation: KHAZZ-biss-en TOORM

Meaning: Literally "cheese-bite tower," i.e., the windows look like bites taken out of a piece of cheese

Chääshändler

Pronunciation: KHAZZ-hand-lehr

Meaning: Cheesemonger

Chind

Pronunciation: KHEENT

Meaning: Child

Chinder

Pronunciation: KHEEN-dair

Meaning: Children

Christstollen

Pronunciation: KRIST-shtohll-len

Meaning: Swiss and German Christmas yeast bread with dried fruits, nuts, spices, and sugar glaze

D

danke vilmal

Pronunciation: DAHN-keh FILL-maal

Meaning: Thank you very much (Swiss German)

Der Schweizerische Beobachter

Pronunciation: dair SHVY-tser-i-sheh beh-OH-bahk-tair

Meaning: A well-known Swiss magazine focusing on consumer rights and social issues

Dichtung

Pronunciation: DEEKH-toong

Meaning: Poetry

Die Leiden des jungen Werthers

Pronunciation: dee LIE-den dess YOONG-en VARE-terss

Meaning: *The Sorrows of Young Werther* is a 1774 novel by Johann Wolfgang von Goethe, written in the form of letters. It tells the story of Werther, a sensitive young man whose unrequited love for a woman named Lotte leads him into despair. The book became a defining work of *Sturm und Drang*, influencing European Romanticism and causing a sensation upon publication.

Du bisch äbe schön.

Pronunciation: doo bish ÄÄ-beh shern

Meaning: You really are beautiful.

Du bist nicht allein.

Pronunciation: doo bisst neekht ah-line

Meaning: You are not alone.

Dukaten

Pronunciation: doo-KAH-ten

Meaning: Gold coins historically used in Europe

E

Emmentaler

Pronunciation: EM-men-tah-lehr

Meaning: A firm, pale yellow cow's milk cheese known for its large, round holes, formed naturally during fermentation. Emmentaler has a smooth, elastic texture and a mild, nutty, slightly sweet flavor that deepens as it ages. Named after the Emmental valley in the canton of Bern, Emmentaler is one of Switzerland's most iconic cheeses.

Er hockt im Gefängnis.

Pronunciation: air hockt im ge-FENG-niss

Meaning: He is sitting in prison.

Erdöpfel

Pronunciation: ÄÄR-depp-fell

Meaning: Potatoes (Swiss German)

F

Fraktur

Pronunciation: frahk-TOOR

Meaning: Gothic blackletter typeface used historically in German-speaking regions

Frau

Pronunciation: frow

Meaning: Woman; Mrs.

Fräulein (obsolete)

Pronunciation: FROY-line

Meaning: Young lady; Miss

Für deine neue Stube.

Pronunciation: fear DYE-neh NOY-eh SHTOO-beh

Meaning: For your new room/home.

G

Gebrüder Grimm

Pronunciation: geh-BREE-dehr GRIMM

Meaning: The Brothers Grimm; nineteenth century collectors of German folktales

Geltwil

Pronunciation: GELT-veel

Meaning: A tiny rural village in the canton of Aargau, situated on a low rise between fields and forest

Gemeinde

Pronunciation: geh-MINE-deh

Meaning: Municipality; local administrative unit

Geographie

Pronunciation: geh-oh-gra-FEE

Meaning: Geography

Geschichte

Pronunciation: geh-SHEEKH-teh

Meaning: History or story

Gipfeli

Pronunciation: GEEP-feh-lee

Meaning: Swiss croissant roll made of buttery dough

Grüezi

Pronunciation: GREE-eh-tsee

Meaning: Hello (Swiss German greeting)

Guete Morge

Pronunciation: GOO-eh-teh MOR-geh

Meaning: Good morning

H

Harzsalbe

Pronunciation: HARTS-saal-beh

Meaning: Resin salve; traditional pine-resin ointment

Heiligaabig

Pronunciation: HYE-leeg-aa-bick

Meaning: Christmas Eve (Swiss German)

Heilkräuter

Pronunciation: HYLE-kroy-tair

Meaning: Medicinal herbs

Heimkehr

Pronunciation: HYME-kair

Meaning: Homecoming

Herr Pfarrer

Pronunciation: hair PFARR-ehr

Meaning: Reverend; parish priest

homoerotisch

Pronunciation: ho-mo-eh-ROH-tish

Meaning: Homoerotic

I

Ich glaub, er het sie nie welle.

Pronunciation: ikh gloub, er het see NEE VELL-leh

Meaning: I think he never wanted her.

J

ja

Pronunciation: yah

Meaning: Yes

K

Kanton

Pronunciation: kahn-TOHN

Meaning: Swiss state/province

Kirche Sankt Antonius

Pronunciation: KEER-kheh sankt an-TOH-nee-oos

Meaning: Church of Saint Anthony

Kirsch

Pronunciation: keersh

Meaning: Cherry brandy; Swiss fruit spirit

Knecht(e)

Pronunciation: KNÄÄKHT(eh)

Meaning: Farmhand(s); servant(s)

Kunstwerke

Pronunciation: KOONST-vair-keh

Meaning: Works of art

L

La Pierraz

Pronunciation: lah pee-RAHZ

Meaning: A small hamlet in the canton of Fribourg, situated in the French-speaking region of the canton

langsam

Pronunciation: LANG-sahm

Meaning: Slow; slowly

Leutknecht

Pronunciation: LOYT-knääkht

Meaning: Senior farmhand; the head laborer on a farm, responsible for overseeing other *Knechte* and carrying out tasks requiring judgment and reliability; a position of trust within the servant hierarchy

Liebe Tochter, komm jetzt heim.

Pronunciation: LEE-uh-beh TOCKH-tehr, kohm yetst hime

Meaning: Dear daughter, come home now.

Lieber Gott

Pronunciation: LEE-uh-behr GOT

Meaning: "Dear God"

Liebes Meiteli

Pronunciation: LEE-uh-bess MIGHT-eh-lee

Meaning: "Dear girl" (Swiss German)

M

Märchen

Pronunciation: MARE-khen

Meaning: Fairy tale

Margueritli

Pronunciation: MAR-geh-reet-lee

Meaning: Little daisy; affectionate diminutive

Marienkirche

Pronunciation: ma-REE-en-keer-kheh

Meaning: Church of Mary

min Schatz

Pronunciation: meen SHAHTS

Meaning: The Swiss German form of *mein Schatz*, the High German term of endearment which literally means "my treasure"; commonly used between spouses or close partners in Switzerland

N

nai

Pronunciation: nye

Meaning: No (Swiss German)

Naturkunde

Pronunciation: nah-TOOR-koon-deh

Meaning: Natural science; nature studies

O

Ottorüthi

Pronunciation: OH-toh-REE-uh-tee

Meaning: The name of the Stirnimann family's home and the vast farm estate that surrounded it in the Luzerner countryside, held by the family for many generations

P

patois

Pronunciation: PAH-twah

Meaning: Local dialect; often refers to Swiss French regional speech

Pelzdecke

Pronunciation: PELTS-dek-keh

Meaning: Fur blanket

Postamt

Pronunciation: POSHT-ahmt

Meaning: Post office

prie-dieu

Pronunciation: pree-DYUH

Literal meaning (French): "pray-God"

Meaning: A small wooden kneeler with a low shelf for resting the elbows or a prayer book, used for private devotion in Catholic homes and churches

Cultural note: Common in nineteenth century rural Catholic Europe; a familiar piece of furniture in confessionals and parish churches like the Marienkirche in Bertiswil

Protokollbuch (PROH-toh-kohl-bookh)

Meaning: The formal bound volume in which sworn legal testimony, minutes of hearings, and official proceedings were recorded. Entries were written carefully, often by a clerk, and became part of the permanent court file.

R

Rahmwähe

Pronunciation: RAHM-veh-eh

Literal meaning: cream tart

Region: Aargau; also found in parts of Luzern

Meaning: A sweet, open-faced tart made with a thin yeast or shortcrust base and filled with lightly sweetened cream, baked until softly set

Reuss

Pronunciation: ROYSS

Meaning: Major Swiss river flowing through central Switzerland

Riesenbaby

Pronunciation: REE-zen-bay-bee

Meaning: "Giant baby"; oversized or unusually large infant

Ringelblumensalbe

Pronunciation: RING-el-bloo-men-sal-beh

Meaning: Calendula salve; traditional herbal healing ointment

Rothenburg

Pronunciation: ROH-tcn-boorg

Meaning: Town in the canton of Luzern

Rüeblichüechli

Pronunciation: REE-eh-blee-KHEE-ekh-lee

Meaning: Small, unfrosted carrot cakes baked in shallow molds, simple and rustic, reflecting the understated style of Swiss farmhouse baking

Rüeblipudding

Pronunciation: REE-eh-blee-POO-ding

Meaning: Sweet carrot pudding

Rüeblisuppe

Pronunciation: REE-eh-blee-SOOP-peh

Meaning: Carrot soup

Rüeblitorte

Pronunciation: REE-eh-blee-TOR-teh

Meaning: A dense, moist Swiss carrot cake made with finely grated carrots, ground almonds, eggs, and a small amount of flour. Unlike American carrot cake, it is not spiced, not frosted, and not layered. Its sweetness comes from the carrots themselves and a scant amount of sugar, giving it a gentle, earthy flavor. The texture is tender and almost marzipan-soft from the almonds. It is traditionally baked in a single round layer and served plain or with a light dusting of powdered sugar.

Rüebliwähe

Pronunciation: REE-eh-blee-VEH-heh

Meaning: Carrot tart/quiche

S

Sbrinz

Pronunciation: SHBREE-intz

Meaning: One of Switzerland's oldest cheeses, Sbrinz is a very hard, slow-ripened cow's milk cheese traditionally aged at least 18 months, often 24–36 months or more. Its texture is dense, brittle, and granular, breaking into small shards rather than slices. The flavor is deep, nutty, and savory, with a concentrated dairy sweetness and a crystalline crunch that comes from long aging.

Schlafzimmer

Pronunciation: SHLAHF-tsim-mehr

Meaning: Bedroom

schön

Pronunciation: SHERN

Meaning: Beautiful; lovely

Schwingen

Pronunciation: SHVING-en

Meaning: A traditional form of Swiss wrestling practiced outdoors on a circular ring of sawdust. Wrestlers wear special canvas breeches and win by throwing an opponent so that both shoulder blades touch the ground.

Cultural note: Schwingen is associated with rural life, alpine festivals, and the values of strength, fairness, and restraint. It was historically practiced by farmers and herdsmen and remains a symbol of Swiss heritage.

sicher

Pronunciation: SEE-kher

Meaning: Sure; safe; certainly

Sie isch nid wie di andere.

Pronunciation: See eesh neet vee dee AHN-dehr-eh

Meaning: She is not like the others.

Sie tuet mer leid.

Pronunciation: see TOO-et mair lide.

Meaning: I feel sorry for her.

Sins

Pronunciation: SINCE

Meaning: town in Swiss canton of Aargau

Siviriez

Pronunciation: see-vee-REE-EH

Meaning: A village in the canton of Fribourg, located in the French-speaking district of Glâne

So ganz allei.

Pronunciation: so GAHNTZ ah-LIE

Meaning: So completely alone.

still

Pronunciation: shteel

Meaning: Quiet; still

Suser

Pronunciation: SOO-sair

Meaning: Partially fermented grape juice; very young wine

Süssmost

Pronunciation: SEE-ess-mosht

Meaning: Sweet cider; unfermented apple juice

T

Tante (Tanti)

Pronunciation: TAHN-teh (TAHN-tee)

Meaning: Aunt (Auntie)

Tilsiter

Pronunciation: TEEL-see-tair

Meaning: A pale yellow, semi-hard cow's milk cheese with a supple, elastic texture and a distinctive, mildly pungent aroma. Tilsiter is dotted with small, irregular holes and has a tangy, slightly sharp flavor that deepens with age.

Tochter

Pronunciation: TOKH-tehr

Meaning: Daughter

Töchterli

Pronunciation: TERK-ter-lee

Meaning: Little daughter; affectionate diminutive in Swiss German

Totenstube

Pronunciation: TOE-ten-SHTOO-beh

Meaning: A small parish building where bodies were kept before burial in nineteenth century Switzerland; the sexton tended the space, and local officials such as a magistrate might conduct inquiries there when a death required examination.

Tracht(en)

Pronunciation: trahkt(en)

Literal meaning: dress, attire, or garb

Meaning: Traditional regional clothing worn in German-speaking areas, including Switzerland. Each canton, valley, or village has its own distinctive *Tracht*, with variations for feast days, church, weddings, and mourning.

Cultural note: In nineteenth century rural Switzerland, one's *Tracht* signaled not only region and community but also marital status, wealth, and religious identity. Women's *Trachten* often included embroidered bodices, aprons, and specific hairstyles. Men's *Trachten* featured waistcoats, jackets, hats, and even earrings unique to the region. Wearing the regional *Tracht* was both a cultural marker and a form of belonging.

U

Und er isch immer so chalt.

Pronunciation: oont air ish IM-mehr so KHALT

Meaning: "And he is always so cold."

Ungeschickt

Pronunciation: OON-ge-shickt

Meaning: Clumsy; awkward

V

Verdingkind(er) (High German)

Pronunciation: fair-DINK-keend(air)

Verdingchind(er) (Swiss German)

Pronunciation: fair-DINK-kheent(air)

Meaning: Contract child(ren); historical term for Swiss indentured child servants placed as farm laborers and domestics

W

Weg

Pronunciation: VEHG

Meaning: Path; way

Weihnachtsguetzli

Pronunciation: VYE-nakhts-goo-etz-lee

Meaning: Christmas cookies

Wilhelm Tell

Pronunciation: VIL-helm TELL

Meaning: An 1804 drama by Friedrich Schiller, based on the Swiss legend of William Tell. Set in the early fourteenth century, the play dramatizes the struggle of the Swiss cantons against Habsburg oppression, culminating in Tell's famous refusal to bow to Gessler's hat and the forced shooting of the apple from his son's head. It is one of the foundational works of Swiss national mythology and a central text in German literature.

Wo isch mini Tanti?

Pronunciation: VO ish MEE-nee TAHN-tee

Meaning: "Where is my auntie?"

Wollmütze

Pronunciation: VOLL-meet-tseh

Meaning: Wool cap

Z

Zmittagässä

Pronunciation: TSMIT-tak-ass-ää

Meaning: The large midday meal

Znachtässä

Pronunciation: TSNAKHT-ASS-ää

Meaning: Supper

Zopf / Zöpfe

Pronunciation: TSOPF/ TSERP-feh

Meaning: Braid(s); braided Swiss yeast bread(s)

Song Lyrics

Da höch uf de Alpe, dem Hüttli nid färn,
da hüet i mini Geissli, da bin i so gern.
Tralalala…
Da lacht mer de Himmel höch über em Schnee
und Matte voll Blüemli, so schön 's will gsee.
Tralalala…

Up high on the alp, not far from the little hut,
there I tend my little goats,
there is where I like to be.
Tralalala…
There the sky smiles at me, high above the snow,
and meadows full of flowers,
so beautiful they long to be seen.
Tralalala…

Lueget, vo Bärgen und Tal
Flieht scho der Sunnestrahl!
Lueget, uf Auen und Matte
Wachse die dunkele Schatte;
D Sunn uf de Bärge no stoht.
O, wie si d Gletscher so rot!

Lueget, do aben a See!
Heimetzuet wendet si ’s Veh;
Loset, wie d Glogge, die schöne,
Fründlig im Moos ’s ertöne.
Chüejerglüt, üseri Lust,
Tuet ’s so wohl i der Brust!

Look—from mountains and valley
the sunlight is already fleeing.
Look—on meadows and pastures
the dark shadows are growing;
the sun still stands on the mountains.
Oh, how red the glaciers are!

Look up there at the lake!
The cattle turn homeward;
listen, how the bells—the beautiful ones—
sound friendly in the moss.
The cowbells, our delight,
do our hearts so much good!

Schlaf, Chindli, schlaf,
der Vater hütet d’Schaf.
Die Mueter schüttlet ’s Bäumeli,
da falle viili Träumeli.
Schlaf, Chindli, schlaf.

Sleep, little child, sleep,
your father is tending the sheep.
Your mother shakes the little tree,
and many little dreams fall down.
Sleep, little child, sleep.

Wen-i nume wüsst,
wo 's Vogel-Lisi wär.
'S Vogel-Lisi chunnt vo Adelbode här.
Adelbode isch im Bärner Oberland.
'S Bärner Oberland isch schö-ö-ön.
'S Oberland, ja 's Oberland,
's Bärner Oberland isch schön.
'S Oberland, ja 's Oberland,
's Bärner Oberland isch schön.

If only I knew
where Bird-Lizzy was.
Bird-Lizzy comes from Adelboden.
Adelboden is in the Bernese Oberland.
The Bernese Oberland is beau-ti-ful.
The Oberland, yes the Oberland—
the Bernese Oberland is beautiful.
The Oberland, yes the Oberland—
the Bernese Oberland is beautiful.

www.ingramcontent.com/pod-product-compliance
Lightning Source LLC
LaVergne TN
LVHW010636110826
845149LV00014B/2849

* 9 7 9 8 9 9 3 3 4 9 1 2 1 *